What could be hotter than a cowboy in June?
How about a cowboy in July, August
and under the mistletoe, too!

New York Times bestselling author
Vicki Lewis Thompson is back in the
Harlequin Blaze lineup for 2014,

and this year she's offering her readers *even more....*

Sons of Chance

Chance isn't just the last name of these rugged
Wyoming cowboys—it's their motto, too!

Saddle up with

#799 RIDING HIGH

(June)

#803 RIDING HARD

(July)

#807 RIDING HOME

(August)

And the sexy conclusion to the
Sons of Chance Christmas series

#823 A LAST CHANCE CHRISTMAS

(December)

Take a chance...on a Chance!

Blaze®

Dear Reader,

When the editors and I first settled on this title, I wasn't sure that it fit the story. I've changed my mind. Drake Brewster might be my most troubled hero so far. He's loaded down with guilt, and he's very hard on himself.

Ah, but he's a charmer, with his Rhett Butler accent and his bad-boy appeal. Those very charms are what got him into hot water, and now he's working to regain the trust of his best friend, Regan. While doing that, he meets Tracy Gibbons, bartender and temporary house sitter for Regan and Regan's fiancée. Tracy is not a Drake Brewster fan.

I'll admit right up front that the folks at the Last Chance Ranch are not enamored of the guy, either. He wronged one of their own, and they're not inclined to be friendly under those circumstances. But you have to hand it to Drake. He sticks it out because that's the only way he'll be able to respect himself as a man.

Welcome to midsummer in Wyoming! The weather is gorgeous, and so is Drake Brewster. Tracy thinks she can resist him, but let me tell you, I couldn't. Come along on another Sons of Chance adventure and see if _you_ can resist this Southern scoundrel! Betcha can't!

Scandalously yours,

Vicki

Riding Hard

—

Vicki Lewis Thompson

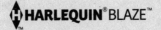

Recycling programs
for this product may
not exist in your area.

ISBN-13: 978-0-373-79807-0

RIDING HARD

Copyright © 2014 by Vicki Lewis Thompson

H HARLEQUIN®

www.Harlequin.com

Printed in U.S.A.

ABOUT THE AUTHOR

New York Times bestselling author Vicki Lewis Thompson's love affair with cowboys started with the Lone Ranger, continued through Maverick and took a turn south of the border with Zorro. She views cowboys as the Western version of knights in shining armor—rugged men who value honor, honesty and hard work. Fortunately for her, she lives in the Arizona desert, where broad-shouldered, lean-hipped cowboys abound. Blessed with such an abundance of inspiration, she only hopes that she can do them justice. Visit her website, www.vickilewisthompson.com.

Books by Vicki Lewis Thompson

HARLEQUIN BLAZE

To everyone who has ever made a mistake and wronged a friend. It's tough to go through life and not do that at least once, so I figure this dedication applies to all of us. Let's forgive ourselves and each other for being human. Oh, and to my dad, from whom I took Psych 101. It was an eye-opener.

Prologue

July 20, 1990

ARCHIE CHANCE WISHED he could be anywhere but here, sitting on a barstool at the Spirits and Spurs. Or, if he had to be here, he wished he hadn't invited his son Jonathan to have a beer with him while the women went shopping at the Shoshone General Store.

The bar was mostly empty, which allowed Archie to hear two strangers at a table about ten feet behind them. Jonathan's tight expression indicated that he could hear it, too. One of the men was reminiscing about a one-night stand he'd enjoyed in Shoshone many years ago with a woman named Diana, a woman who sounded a hell of a lot like Jonathan's ex-wife.

Archie pushed away his half-empty beer glass. "Let's shove off."

Jonathan shook his head. "Not yet."

"Look, does it really matter what—"

"Yes."

Archie understood. In Jonathan's shoes, he would

have wanted to know, too. Diana had abandoned Jonathan and their young son, Jack, ten years ago and had severed all ties with the family. Archie wouldn't be surprised if she'd also had affairs during their unhappy marriage.

Archie had heard enough. Way too much, in fact. The woman named Diana had mentioned being married to a surly cowboy whose family owned a big spread outside of town.

Archie sipped his beer and stared straight ahead, because he didn't know what else to do. After what seemed like years, the two men left.

When Jonathan finally spoke, his voice was husky. "I was, you know."

Archie turned, not sure what his son was admitting to. "You were what?"

"Surly."

"Well, you had good reason to be, damn it. She was a difficult woman. Probably still is." Archie wasn't supposed to overreact to things and get his blood pressure up, but he couldn't help it.

"She was unhappy. I had no patience with her."

"Because you didn't love her." *None of us did.*

"I…" Jonathan picked up his glass, then put it back down. "No, I didn't love her. I realize that now, because of Sarah. I'm still not very patient, but when she reminds me of that, I don't get mad. I try harder. I'm lucky to have her, and I don't want to mess up a good thing."

Archie's eyes grew moist. He'd developed an embarrassing tendency to get choked up over his family lately. Nelsie assured him that grandpas were allowed, but he thought it was unmanly. He cleared his throat. "You're lucky to have each other."

Jonathan glanced at him. "Just like you and Mom. I always wanted what you two have, and now, I have it."

"Yep." Aw, hell, now he was tearing up again thinking about Nelsie, the love of his life. He took a long swallow of his beer and hoped his son didn't think he was turning into a sentimental old fool. Once he had himself under control, he looked over at Jonathan. "Hey, how about another beer? We can toast the ladies."

That boy's smile always could light up a room. "Great idea, Dad."

In nothing flat, Archie went from wanting to get the hell out of the bar to wanting to stay forever. Funny how a situation that started out as a disaster could end up turning into something pretty damned wonderful, after all.

1

DRAKE BREWSTER WAS used to women liking him, but Tracy Gibbons, the beautiful bartender at Spirits and Spurs, clearly didn't. Oh, she was polite enough when she served him a beer, but her smile was mostly fake, as if she was forcing herself because he was a customer. He even knew why she didn't like him, but that didn't help much. When he thought about her reasons, he had to agree they were legitimate.

In point of fact, he wasn't particularly popular with anyone in Shoshone, Wyoming. He was the guy who'd had sex with his best friend's fiancée six months ago. On Christmas Eve. Apparently word had gotten out, and now everyone avoided him like a skunk at a Fourth of July picnic.

That very same best friend, Regan O'Connelli, happened to be quite popular in this neighborhood. Well connected, too. After severing his business relationship with Drake back in Virginia, as well he should have, he'd gone into partnership with Shoshone veterinarian Nick Chance. It had been a logical move since one of Regan's sisters had married Nick's brother Gabe, and another had married Nick's brother-in-law Alex. Getting hooked into the Chance family opened all kinds of doors around here, apparently.

Getting crossways with the Chances, though, slammed those doors shut in a man's face. Regan, who swore he'd forgiven Drake for the fiasco with Jeannette on that fateful Christmas Eve, said Drake should give people time. They'd come around.

Three weeks into his stay, Drake wasn't so sure. The deep freeze was still on, except for Regan and his new fiancée, Lily King. Drake gave Lily much of the credit for Regan's willingness to forgive and forget. She was a softhearted woman.

In fact, her soft heart had nearly been her downfall when she'd bought Peaceful Kingdom, a horse-rescue operation outside of town, and had accepted every unwanted animal dumped at her feet. Besides the horses, she'd taken in two potbellied pigs and several chickens. Regan had saved her from herself, and in the process, they'd fallen in love. She encouraged Drake to visit as often as he could, but he didn't want to wear out his welcome. Couples in love needed alone time.

That should have fit right in with his plans. Before leaving Virginia, he'd put his vet practice in the hands of a colleague and hadn't specified when he'd be back. Then he'd rented an isolated cabin just outside the boundary of the Last Chance Ranch so that he could make amends with Regan and take a few weeks to re-evaluate his life.

He'd imagined long solo hikes and intense periods of soul-searching would help him figure out how he'd veered so off track that he'd gone to bed with his best friend's girl. His life couldn't be working if he could do something that disloyal, and he'd hoped for some insights.

Surprisingly, his jealousy of Regan's self-confidence had been one of his issues. Realizing he'd set out to sabotage his friend's sense of self-worth was an ugly truth he'd had trouble facing. But he had faced it, and consequently he and Regan were okay.

His period of self-examination had yielded another nugget of wisdom. He wasn't into long solo hikes and intense periods of soul-searching. He was a sociable type, a Southerner who loved to talk, and he craved the company of others. But except for Regan and Lily, nobody within a thirty-mile radius craved *his* company, and that sucked.

Yet here he was, anyway, sitting on a barstool at the Spirits and Spurs during happy hour trying not to look as lonely as he felt. A few people had said hello, but then they'd gone back to talking to whomever they'd come with. Nobody seemed interested in a prolonged encounter with the guy who'd wronged Regan O'Connelli.

Tracy made a circuit of the bar area, her dark hair shining, her red lipstick glossy and inviting. She glanced at his nearly empty glass. "Another round?"

Drake considered giving up and going back to the cabin but couldn't make himself do it. "Sure. Thanks."

"Coming up." That fake smile flashed again.

He watched her walk away. She had the perfect figure for jeans, and he'd noticed other guys checking out her ass. But someone with his hound-dog reputation couldn't be caught doing it, so instead he studied her hair. It was up in some arrangement that kept it out of the way, but he pictured how it would look loose. It might reach halfway down her back, at least, and sway as she moved. Nice.

He didn't want her to see him staring like some wet-behind-the-ears doofus, so he grabbed the menu out of its holder. Then he proceeded to scan the offerings as if fascinated by what he'd found, although he knew them by heart.

"Here you go."

He glanced up, as if he hadn't noticed her coming toward him. "Thank you, ma'am." The beer foam was perfectly symmetrical. He raised the glass and admired it. "Very pretty." He meant the compliment for her, but he could always claim he'd been talking about the head on his beer.

"Thanks." She didn't quite roll her eyes, but she looked as if she wanted to. She gestured toward the menu. "Would you like something to eat?"

He wasn't hungry, but picking up a menu was a classic signal and there wasn't much in the refrigerator at the cabin. "I would, indeed. What do you recommend?"

She paused, confusion shadowing her brown eyes. "Don't you want your usual burger and fries?"

"I find myself wantin' something different." That she'd noticed his ordering pattern meant nothing, of course. Any good server would do that. But it pleased him, anyway.

"Well, then…you might try the barbecued-pork sandwich. Lots of people like that."

"Do you like it?"

She hesitated, as if not wanting to give him personal information. "I'm partial to the burgers here," she said at last.

"So am I. I'll stick with my usual, after all."

"Okay. I'll put in the order." She started to turn away.

"Tracy?"

When she looked back at him, her expression was guarded. "What?"

He tried to remember if he'd ever used her name, although he'd known it for days. Maybe not. Southerners tended to use *ma'am* most of the time. He took a deep breath, finally ready to tackle this situation head-on. "I've been coming in here quite a bit lately."

"Yes, you have." She didn't seem particularly happy about it, either.

"And you're always polite to me."

"I certainly hope so. If I'm not nice to the customers, I would probably get fired."

"I appreciate that, but I'll bet there are some customers you look forward to serving and some you don't."

Her gaze became shuttered. "I'm grateful for any and all customers who come through the door. Without customers, Spirits and Spurs wouldn't be in business."

"Nice speech. I admire your dedication. But the fact remains that you don't like me."

She opened her mouth as if to reply. Then she closed it again.

"Don't worry. I'm not going to complain to anyone about it." He sighed. "Hell, you're in the majority around here when it comes to holdin' a bad opinion of me. But nobody will say it to my face. They're unfailingly polite and then they act like I have a contagious disease."

"I'm Regan's friend." Her gaze turned very cold. "I'm also friends with his sisters. If you think my attitude is chilly, you should try having a conversation with Morgan, Tyler or Cassidy."

"Yeah, I figured that wouldn't work out, so I haven't tried."

"I know everything's supposed to be hunky-dory between you and Regan. Lily told me all is well, but she's the kind of person who would make excuses for a serial killer."

"A serial killer? Isn't that a bit harsh?"

"I know you haven't actually killed anyone, but you betrayed your *best friend*." Anger kindled in her brown eyes. "If you ask me, Regan's letting you off *way* too easy." Then she blushed and glanced away. "Sorry. I get a little worked up when I talk about this. It's really none of my business."

He thought she was mighty pretty when she was worked up, but he wisely didn't say so. "I get the impression that it's everybody's business around here."

She didn't deny it, probably because she couldn't. When she looked at him again, her gaze was disconcertingly direct. "Why stay, then? You patched things up with Regan, so why not go back to Virginia where… where you're from."

Where you belong. Although she didn't say the words, they hung in the air. Except he didn't belong in Virginia anymore. He couldn't explain why, but the thought of returning to his old life made him shudder.

Whoever he'd been back there wasn't the man he wanted to be here and now. The location might have nothing to do with it, but he wasn't going to take the chance that he'd fall into his old patterns.

He shrugged. "I must be a glutton for punishment."

Something shifted in her expression. It became more open, and unless he was mistaken, she seemed genuinely interested in him for the first time ever. "I see."

"What do you see?"

"That you're doing some kind of penance."

"I wouldn't put it that way." The assessment made him uncomfortable. He wasn't a masochist or a martyr.

"You just called yourself a glutton for punishment."

"That's an expression, something folks say. It doesn't mean that I—"

"Hey, Drake!"

Intensely grateful for the interruption, he swiveled to face Regan, who came toward him looking like the seasoned cowboy he'd become, complete with boots, worn jeans and a ten-gallon hat. Drake had bought some boots and a couple of pairs of jeans that still looked new. He was holding off buying a hat. He couldn't say why.

He held out a hand to Regan. "Hey, buddy! What's up?"

"Not much." Regan shook hands, but the dark eyes he'd inherited from his Italian mother moved quickly from Drake to Tracy. "Am I interrupting?"

"Nope!" Tracy waved her order pad. "I have to put in Drake's food order and check on my other customers. Can I bring you something?"

"I'll take a draft when you have a minute. I actually came in to see you, but I wanted to ask Drake a favor, too, so this is perfect."

"All righty, then. I'll be back." She hurried toward the kitchen.

Regan slid onto a barstool on Drake's right. "*Did* I interrupt something? You both looked mighty serious."

"Not really. I made a dumb remark and she picked up on it."

"What'd you say?"

"She wondered why I'm stayin' here when nobody likes me, and I—"

"Hang on." Regan shoved back the brim of his Stetson. "She actually said that nobody likes you? That doesn't sound like Tracy."

"Actually I'm the one who said that, but she didn't disagree with me. You have to admit I'm not the toast of Shoshone, Wyoming."

"Maybe not yet."

"Maybe not ever. You have loyal friends who don't forgive easily. I understand that. Tracy asked a logical question, and I gave her a flip answer."

"Like what?"

"I said maybe I was a glutton for punishment."

"Oh, boy." Regan chuckled. "I'll bet that got her attention."

"It did, but why are you so sure it would?"

"She's studying to be a psychologist, but don't mention that I told you."

"Why? What's the big secret?"

"It's not actually a secret. As you've discovered, gossip is a favorite pastime in this little town."

Drake pretended to be shocked. "Really?"

"Yeah, yeah. Anyway, people kind of know because she keeps her books behind the bar and studies when it's not busy in here. But she's not ready to announce it to the world. I think she's worried that she doesn't have the intellectual chops to pull it off."

"You're kidding." Drake thought of her efficiency and the intelligence shining in those brown eyes. "She's smart as a whip. Anyone can see that."

"Yeah, but nobody in her family has ever set foot on a college campus. She's only taken online classes so far, and she probably doesn't want to make a big deal out of this and then fail."

"She won't fail."

Regan smiled. "Spoken like a man who always knew he'd end up with a degree and a profession. She doesn't have that kind of background, and she has doubts."

"Well, she shouldn't, but I see your point." He paused. "Wait, are you saying she was trying to psychoanalyze me? That's all I need."

"At least it would be free."

Drake skewered his friend with a look and discovered Regan was working hard not to laugh. "It's not funny, damn it. I might need a shrink, but I sure as hell don't need a shrink in training. I'm messed up enough without accidentally gettin' the wrong advice."

"I wouldn't discount Tracy's insights. She's spent a lot of hours behind this bar, and she has a knack for reading people. She can't officially hang out a shingle until she graduates and gets licensed, but she has excellent instincts."

"Mmm." Drake didn't like this discussion any more than the one he'd been having with Tracy. He took another swig of beer.

"Look, you told me you wanted to get your head on

straight while you're here. You could do worse than talk things over with Tracy."

"I beg to differ." Drake sighed. "Besides, aren't psychologists supposed to be nonjudgmental?"

"Yeah, I suppose so."

"Then Tracy didn't get the memo. She believes what I did was heinous and she's not cuttin' me any slack. I hardly think she's the person to help me."

"Okay, maybe not. I'm not sure why, but I know infidelity is a hot button for her."

Drake winced as he always did when that word came up. He'd willingly participated in an act of infidelity. Even though liquor had been involved, which created some sort of lame excuse, the sharpness of what he'd done couldn't be filed down, and it still cut deep.

"So I guess it's not such a good idea," Regan said. "Forget I mentioned it."

"I surely will. Besides, there's another factor that makes the idea a nonstarter."

"What?"

"I think she's hot."

"Oh." Regan's glance slid past Drake and focused on a spot over his shoulder. "Here she comes. I'd advise you to keep that information to yourself."

"Don't worry. I'm not about to make myself vulnerable to a woman who thinks I'm pond scum."

"She doesn't think that."

"I'll guarantee she does." Drake swiveled his stool back around and smiled at Tracy.

Her mouth responded with an obligatory upward tilt, but the rest of her face was devoid of emotion. Then she looked at Regan, and everything changed. "Here's your

beer and some peanuts in case you get the munchies."
She'd never offered Drake peanuts.

"Thanks." Regan pushed the bowl toward Drake.
"Want some?"

"Don't mind if I do." He'd show Tracy that he wasn't
too proud to eat Regan's free peanuts.

Tracy lingered in front of Regan. "Can I get you
anything else?"

"Nope, this is great. But I have a big favor to ask."

"What's that?"

"Nick's going to a conference in Washington, D.C.
next week and he's taking Dominique because she's
never been to the Capitol. At the last minute he asked
if Lily and I wanted to come along. The women can pal
around and sightsee while we're in meetings. I wondered
if you'd be willing to house-sit again while we're gone."

"Of course! I'll have to make sure my hours here will
mesh with feeding the critters, but that shouldn't be a
problem. I can trade off with somebody if necessary."

Drake was flabbergasted. And more than a little hurt.
A couple of weeks ago Regan and Lily had taken a two-
day vacation and had asked Tracy to house-sit. When
Drake found out, he'd told them to ask him next time.

He was a vet, for crying out loud, so he could easily
deal with the animals. He also had zip going on. Instead
Regan had asked a busy person who already had a full-
time job and was studying to become a psychologist.

"Great!" Regan gave Tracy a big old smile. "Same
deal as before. Don't accept any new animals."

"I won't."

"And because we'll be gone for so long, I've arranged
for a vet in Jackson to take the routine calls at the office

and help you out if you need it. But I'm hoping Drake will consider stepping in if there's an emergency." He glanced over at Drake. "Would you be able to do that, just until the guy from Jackson can get down here?"

"Uh, sure. Be glad to." He could have handled everything, if Regan had bothered to ask.

"Thanks. I really appreciate it. I keep most of my supplies in my truck, and it'll be parked beside the house. Tracy, if you have any problems at all, call Drake. He's an excellent vet."

Drake had been so busy having his feelings hurt that he hadn't seen that coming. Tracy hadn't either, judging from the way her eyes widened and her mouth dropped open.

"You'll need my number, then." He enjoyed saying it, even if she didn't enjoy hearing it.

"Uh, yeah, I guess I will. But I'm sure nothing will happen."

"Probably not, but just in case, you'd better take it. Call or text anytime."

"Right." She scribbled the number he gave her on her order pad.

"Then we're all set." Regan beamed at them. "We might stay a couple of extra days, if that's okay with you two."

You two. Drake was amused by the way Regan had neatly linked them up. Tracy probably hated it. "I'm fine with y'all staying longer," he said. "How about you, Tracy?"

"Uh, sure. Just let me know in advance so I can adjust my hours. Listen, I'd better get back to my custom-

ers. Drake's burger and fries should be up by now, too."
She quickly made her escape.

Drake wasn't ready to let the issue go. "I could have
handled all of it," he said in a low voice. "I believe I
told you that the last time you asked her."

"I know, and I was keeping you in reserve if she
had other plans. But she said yes, probably because she
needs the money for school. I figured she did."

"Oh, you're paying her." Drake felt better. "I didn't
realize that."

"We're absolutely paying her. We paid her last time,
too. There's a lot of work involved. I wouldn't expect
anyone to do it for free."

"I would've."

"And that's one of the reasons I didn't want to ask
you. I knew you wouldn't take any money for it, and
Tracy will." Regan studied him. "You do realize that
I'm not mad at you anymore, right?"

"Yeah, I do." His chuckle sounded hollow. "Sadly,
I'm still riddled with guilt."

"Well, hell, dude. Get over it." Regan tossed a peanut in his mouth.

"Believe me, I'm trying. Taking care of your place
for free while y'all are gone would've helped, but I get
why you asked Tracy. I wouldn't want to deprive her
of a chance to earn extra money."

"And I hoped you'd be her backup if she has any issues. Legally I can't pay you since you're not licensed in
Wyoming, but I know you don't care about the money."

"Nope. Don't worry about anything. I'll keep an eye
on the medical side of things, but you do realize Tracy
hates the thought of having to call on me."

"She won't hate it if one of the horses gets sick. Everything went fine last time, but we were only a couple of hours away if she'd needed us. Frankly, I wouldn't have agreed to a cross-country trip if I couldn't count on you in the event of a problem."

"I'll surely do that. But now I wish I hadn't told you that I think she's hot."

"Why?"

Drake looked away. "Because I don't want you to think I'll take this as a golden opportunity."

"Good God. You are not only riddled with guilt, you're drowning in it. You and Tracy are consenting adults. I like you both. What happens between you has nothing to do with me unless you scare the horses."

Drake glanced over to find Regan grinning. "I promise not to do that."

"Then everything else is up for grabs."

Drake didn't think so. Tracy had a poor opinion of him, and it would take a miracle to change her mind.

2

As THE NOONDAY sun beat down on her, Tracy stared at the pregnant Appaloosa that the sad-looking cowboy had insisted on unloading despite Tracy's protests. She was a striking mare with a Dalmatian-like coat. Her mane and tail mixed strands of black and white into a soft gray. Tracy instantly wanted to take in this lovely creature.

But her instructions from Regan and Lily had been crystal clear. Just like the first time she house-sat for them, she wasn't supposed to accept any animals while they were gone. "I'm sorry." She kept her tone friendly but firm. "I'm not authorized to admit any animals this week. Perhaps you'd like to come back at the end of the month when the owners are here."

"Can't wait that long, ma'am. I can't feed her no more. I've run through the money I got from selling my stud and I can't find work." The man could have been anywhere from thirty to fifty years old, but he'd obviously lived a hard life judging from his weathered skin and resigned expression.

"I wish I could help, but—"

"I came *this close* to selling Dottie to a guy in Jackson, but he wouldn't have treated her right. I'm beggin' you to take her."

"If she's valuable, and I can see that she probably is, surely you can find someone you trust who would buy her."

"No time. Got an eviction notice for the place I rent yesterday. I'm out of feed for Dottie and out of options. I heard about this rescue operation and figured it was my last hope to put her somewheres she'd be looked after."

Tracy heard the desperation in his voice. This wasn't some jerk who'd grown tired of his responsibility. The man genuinely loved his mare and was terrified something bad would happen to her because he'd lost the ability to provide for her.

Last time Tracy had taken care of Peaceful Kingdom, all twelve of the barn's stalls had been occupied. But Regan and Lily had worked hard to adopt out the young and healthy horses. Six of the residents were so old and feeble they'd live at Peaceful Kingdom forever. Two others needed to learn some manners before they'd be ready to go. Four stalls stood empty.

It wasn't her place to fill even one of them. She'd be acting against orders if she did. But this situation tugged at her heart. She met the cowboy's gaze and made her decision. "I'll take her."

His shoulders dropped and his eyes grew suspiciously moist. "Thank you, ma'am. Thank you."

His gruff tone choked her up a little, too. "Let me get the form for you to fill out." She hurried back to the house and returned in a flash with a clipboard, an intake form and a pen before doubts could change her mind. She held them out to him. "We need some information for our records." Regan and Lily would understand. They had to.

If possible, he looked even more miserable. "Sorry, ma'am. I can't."

For a split second she thought he was refusing to fill out the form, but then she realized he was illiterate on top of his other problems. "No worries. I'll do it. Just tell me what to write."

The man's name was Jerry Rankin. He'd bought Dottie as a foal ten years ago, when times were good for him. Once Tracy started asking questions, Jerry offered all sorts of details that weren't on the form.

When he'd been blessed with steady work, he'd bought an Appaloosa stallion with plans to start a breeding operation. His wife had handled the paperwork, and all had gone well. They'd bred the horses and sold three foals. But then his wife had died after an illness that ate up their savings, and he'd lost his job.

When Tracy finished filling out the form, she glanced up. "Can you sign your name?"

"My wife taught me that much." He took the clipboard and pen and painstakingly wrote his name in awkward block letters.

"Thank you, Mr. Rankin."

"Jerry's good enough."

"Jerry, then."

"I surely do appreciate this." He handed over the lead rope, but the mare stayed right by his side. Then he dug in the pocket of his worn jeans. "I ain't got nothin' but change, but I'll give you what I—"

"No, no. That's okay. You keep it." She felt like offering him money, instead. "I don't know if you've checked into this, but the county has programs if you find yourself...a little short."

He nodded. "I know. I might consider that." He returned the coins to his pocket. "Much obliged to you for taking Dottie. That's a load off my mind."

"You're welcome."

"She's a good horse."

"I'm sure she is."

He stroked the Appaloosa's nose. "You be a good girl for the lady, you hear?"

The mare turned her head and nudged his chest.

"I know. I'll miss you, too. It's for the best."

Tracy swallowed a lump in her throat. "Mr. Rankin... Jerry, she'll be right here. If things should start looking up for you, you can come and get her."

He touched the brim of his battered cowboy hat. "That's right nice of you, ma'am." His voice grew husky. "I'll...I'll keep it in mind." He stroked Dottie's nose once more and started for his truck.

"We'll take good care of her," Tracy called after him.

He didn't respond other than to give a brief nod.

The mare turned her head to gaze after him. Then she nickered.

Tracy feared she might start bawling. Apparently she wasn't cut out for this kind of work. She hoped that dealing with people problems turned out to be less emotionally difficult than dealing with animal problems. Otherwise she wouldn't be a very effective psychologist.

Dottie nickered again as the truck and trailer pulled through the gate.

"Come on, girl." Tracy rubbed the mare's silky neck. "Time for a cozy stall and some oats. I'll bet you haven't had any of those in a while." She exerted firm pressure on the lead rope and Dottie followed her obediently to the barn, proving that she was, as Jerry had said, a good horse. Tracy settled her into an empty stall at the far end of the barn and gave her the promised bucket of oats. The mare ate them greedily.

"Okay, this was a good decision...I guess." Tracy leaned on the stall door and watched the mare. She was a good-looking horse, the color of rich cream with a rump speckled in black.

"The thing is, Dottie, I know nothing about prenatal care, and I'll bet you could use a few vitamins and minerals." Gazing at the horse's extended belly, she realized she didn't know how far along the mare was. It hadn't been on the form, but she should have thought to ask, anyway.

She considered her options. She could call the vet in Jackson, who would charge a pretty penny to evaluate the mare and prescribe vitamins. She'd been instructed not to accept any animals, so adding an expensive vet visit seemed wrong when she could get the same services for free. All she had to do was call Drake Brewster.

Yeah, right. So easy. Just call up Mr. Gorgeous-But-Untrustworthy and ask him to give his professional opinion on the pregnant mare she'd just taken in against Regan and Lily's specific instructions. She wondered if Drake would mention that she'd overstepped. Probably not, considering his history. Talk about overstepping. He'd written the book on it.

Still, she knew Regan and Lily would want her to call Drake instead of the vet in Jackson. No question about that. If she phoned Drake, he'd come right over. The guy didn't seem to have a full schedule. And he'd be very nice. Charming, even. Of course he was charming or he wouldn't have been able to talk Regan's fiancée into going to bed with him.

At least, Tracy assumed that's how it had gone. She couldn't imagine a woman cheating on Regan unless she'd had too much to drink and had been wooed by a master of seduction like Drake Brewster. Tracy was outraged by what he'd done. She was disapproving, scandalized and…so embarrassing to admit, titillated.

Face it, the man was breathtaking. She'd heard his disreputable story before he'd ever walked into Spirits and Spurs. Everybody in town had, and they were all ready to give Drake the cold shoulder and condemn Regan's fiancée in absentia. But when Drake finally did come into the bar, Tracy forgave Regan's fiancée immediately.

Not many women would be able to resist a full-court press by someone who looked like *that*. Those sleepy green eyes and a smile full of equal parts mischief and sin would make short work of any girl's virtuous resolve. Pair those attributes with broad shoulders, slim hips and coffee-colored hair with a slight tendency to curl, and you had the promise of intense pleasure wrapped up in one yummy serving of manhood.

She certainly didn't *want* to be attracted to him. God, no! Too bad. She was, anyway. Her line of defense had been a cool, distant manner. Apparently it had worked, because he thought she didn't like him. Actually, he was right about that. She didn't like him, or more precisely, she didn't like the kind of person who would betray his best friend.

Yet whenever Drake came within five feet of her, she tingled. At the three-foot mark, she burned. She'd made sure he never got any closer than that, because she didn't want to find out what would happen. She was afraid she'd turn into a hypocrite.

So calling him about the mare presented a problem. She'd have to keep her distance when he showed up. No one would ever need to know about her inconvenient case of lust. She'd taken in the pregnant mare, and consequently she had to do the next logical thing and summon Drake.

Pulling her phone from her pocket, she located his number. Her pulse accelerated at the thought of talking to him. That was the other thing about Drake. He had a voice like aged bourbon, complete with the soft drawl of a man born and raised in Virginia. It was a bedroom voice if she'd ever heard one. He sounded like effing Rhett Butler.

He answered quickly. "Hey there, Miss Tracy. Problems?"

She hadn't counted on the effect of his voice murmuring in her ear, and she felt chills down her spine.

She brought the phone to waist level and punched the speaker button. "Not a problem, exactly. I took in a pregnant mare today."

"You're kidding."

"I couldn't turn her away. The guy is down to his last dime, but he refused to sell her to someone he thought might mistreat her. He chose to bring her here instead of taking the money, which he obviously needs. He's being evicted and he has no job."

"Did you give him a job?"

His compassionate suggestion impressed her. "No, but that's a fabulous idea. Obviously I can't hire him, but Regan and Lily might. That's assuming we can find him again. We have no permanent address or phone number. Just a name."

"In a place where everybody seems to know everybody, that should be enough. How far along is the mare?"

"I didn't think to ask. But I assume she needs special care, and I didn't want to bring the vet down from Jackson and incur extra expense." She paused to see if he'd volunteer his services.

"She might be fine for a week or so."

Damn him, he was going to make her ask. "She might, but I would feel terrible if she or the foal had issues because I didn't give her what she needs. Besides, it would be nice to know her approximate due date."

"True, but Regan can figure that out when he gets home."

Tracy's frustration grew. "What if she's ready to pop?"

His laugh was like warm maple syrup. "Is that your roundabout way of inviting me over to take a look?"

"I'd appreciate it if you'd come and examine her." She injected as much formality into the statement as she could muster.

"I'll be right there."

Her stupid adrenaline level spiked. "Thank you. Bye." She disconnected quickly. Brisk and efficient. That was the key. So. ehow she'd continue to strike that note.

Now that he was on his way, she was suddenly concerned about how she looked. She'd showered this morning, but she hadn't bothered with makeup and her hair was pulled back in a simple ponytail. Whenever Drake had seen her at Spirits and Spurs she'd been wearing makeup and a cute hair arrangement. To her secret shame, she'd spent more time on her appearance since he'd started coming into the bar.

How sick was that? She didn't really want to ittract his attention. Well, apparently she did, and now he'd arrive and discover what she looked like au naturel. That was a good thing. No matter how much she longed to race into the house and slap on some lipstick, she would *not*.

Instead she picked up a brush and went to work on Dottie's speckled coat. To Jerry Rankin's credit, Dottie didn't look as if she needed to be brushed, but Tracy did it, anyway. Then she combed out the black-and-white mane and tail, all the while talking to the mare and telling her what a beautiful baby she would have.

Dottie stood quietly and seemed to enjoy the attention, but she'd maneuvered herself so that she could look out the stall door as if watching for Jerry to return. At one point she moved her head to gaze at Tracy as if trying to decide why this strange person had replaced her old buddy.

"He would have kept you if he could," Tracy said. "Bringing you here was an act of love. He didn't want you to fall into bad hands, or to suffer because he wasn't able to take care of you properly."

The explanation seemed to help. Dottie heaved a big horsey sigh and lowered her head to nibble on the straw scattered at her feet.

Tracy wondered if the mare was still hungry. After all, she was eating for two. What Tracy knew about such things would fit inside a bottle cap. She really did need Drake's advice.

As if her thoughts had conjured him up, she heard him enter the barn, his boot heels clicking on the wooden floor. She hurried over to the stall door and glanced quickly down the aisle. Sunlight streamed into the barn, outlining his manly physique in gold. He'd taken to wearing Western clothes recently, and they suited him. Boy, did they ever suit him.

She needed to gather her wits, so she didn't call out to him. Hoping he hadn't noticed her, she went back to brushing Dottie. For someone who had vowed to remain cool and distant, she sure had a lot of heat pouring through her veins. She drew in a deep breath and let it out slowly.

"Tracy? Are you in here?" His rich voice echoed in the rafters.

"Down here, last stall on the left." Damn, but her hands were shaking. This was not good.

"Thanks. I tried the house, but you didn't answer the door." His footsteps came closer. "My eyes aren't quite adjusted to the light."

She glanced up, and there he was, six-foot-something of testosterone-fueled male. His Western shirt emphasized the breadth of his shoulders. He wasn't wearing a cowboy hat, and she didn't think she'd ever seen him wearing one. She wondered about that. Most cowboy wannabes couldn't wait to show up in a hat.

When he opened the stall door, she realized her mistake. Jumpiness aside, she should have walked out to meet him. Then she could have let him go in the stall alone. Instead he was about to come in with her.

Unless she engineered a little do-si-do with him and then made her escape looking like a frightened rabbit, she was stuck here. Her three-foot limit was about to be violated, and she didn't know what to do about it.

He caught sight of the mare and let out a low whistle. "She's a beauty."

"I know." Her plan of maintaining a formal distance crumbled. She'd been through an emotional experience and she needed to talk about Jerry and his willingness to sacrifice for Dottie. "I'll bet he could have sold her, but he couldn't find the right buyer in time. I was touched by the fact he was choosy when he couldn't afford to be."

"Yeah, that's damned noble." He entered the stall and smiled at her. "For the record, I'm glad you followed your instincts and took her. Those instructions didn't anticipate a mare like this showing up."

Five feet, still just the tingle. "I'm sure she was the one bright spot in the guy's life. I hope Regan and Lily are ready to take on some help and that we can find him again if they are."

"I'd say there's an excellent chance that will work out."

"Then I'll think positive, too." *Three feet, starting to burn.*

"What's her name?"

"Dottie." She sounded breathless, but maybe he'd think she had allergies. She backed up a foot and hoped the move wasn't too obvious.

Drake laughed. "Appropriate. Hi, Dottie." He held out a hand, palm up. She saw he was holding a peeled baby carrot.

The mare snuffled against his open palm and took the carrot. She crunched it between her strong teeth as Drake ran his hands over her neck, her shoulders and her distended belly.

God help her, Tracy followed the path of that gentle stroking. After all the promises to herself that she'd ignore his considerable sex appeal, she couldn't help imagining how those hands would feel caressing a woman. No, not just *a* woman. Her.

She wanted to feel the magic of those hands. And they would be magic. Watching him with the horse was evidence of that. She longed to experience that lazy, sensual touch....

No, she didn't! What was wrong with her? She was

falling under his spell. He probably didn't even realize he was casting one. Sensuality was instinctive with him, it seemed. He was surrounded by an invisible magnetic field, and just like that, she'd been drawn back into the three-foot zone.

"A more thorough exam would tell us for sure." Drake continued to stroke the horse. Typical female, Dottie was eating it up. "But from a preliminary evaluation, I'd say she's less than a month from delivering." He glanced over his shoulder at Tracy. "You weren't far off. She's almost ready to pop."

"Good grief." She placed a hand over her racing heart, which now had two reasons to be out of control—lust and terror. "I don't want that happening on my watch."

"You probably won't have to deal with it." His voice was soothing.

She wondered if veterinarians cultivated a bedside manner. If so, Drake had a hell of a good one. "But I might have to deal with it, right?"

"Mothers about to give birth are always unpredictable. But don't worry. I can drive out here at a moment's notice. If she goes into labor, you won't have to handle it alone."

"Good." The rush of gratitude, mixed with the sensual feelings he inspired, became a potent combination. She struggled to remember why she didn't like this man. Oh, yes. He'd betrayed his best friend. No matter how welcome his presence was at the moment, he'd chosen to trade years of friendship for immediate pleasure.

"She'll need some prenatal supplements."

Tracy fought to concentrate on what he was saying instead of imagining him naked in her bed. "Supplements. Right."

"I'll order them from a company I have an account with. My professional discount will keep the cost down."

"Good. Thank you. I honestly didn't consider all the ramifications of this. Assuming her foal is okay, and I hope to heck it is, I've actually accepted two horses."

"True." He lightly scratched Dottie's neck, and her eyelids drifted down in obvious ecstasy. Lucky horse. "But I don't think you have to worry about Regan and Lily. They'll support what you've done."

"I hope so." But she wasn't terribly worried about Regan and Lily. They were animal lovers and would understand. The foal might even be fun for them.

But she was extremely worried about the inevitable contact with Drake and her increasingly intense reaction to his proximity. She had strong principles. Surely a sweet-talking Southerner wouldn't cause her to abandon those principles. *Surely not.*

3

DRAKE WAS PROUD of himself. He'd examined the mare and interacted with Tracy as if he had no interest in her whatsoever. Then he'd left after promising to order the supplements online the minute he got back to his cabin and his computer.

Driving home, he congratulated himself on being a perfect gentleman the whole time. Not once had he given in to the temptation to flirt with her. For him that was a major victory. Regan clearly thought that he would hit on Tracy if given the chance, and he was determined to prove that he could resist that urge.

It hadn't been easy. Before today, they'd always been separated by a massive wooden bar and surrounded by other people. This had been a far more intimate encounter, and she'd looked quite accessible in her T-shirt and jeans, no makeup, and her hair held by a little elastic thing that could be pulled off in no time.

At the bar he'd experienced a jolt of desire whenever he looked at her lipstick-covered mouth. She liked to wear red, and those lips had beckoned him, even when he'd known her smile meant nothing. Logically he shouldn't have been even more turned on by the soft pink of her bare mouth, but he had been. Seeing her like that made him think of how she'd look first thing in the morning. He yearned for the privilege of waking up next to Tracy Gibbons.

He yearned for what would precede that moment, too. He was a fair judge of women. Make that an *excellent* judge of women. Tracy had a lot of passion buried in her.

And here was the kicker. She was as hot for him as he was for her. During his visits to the Spirits and Spurs, she'd fooled him with her remote attitude and obvious disapproval. He thought she still disapproved of him. But underneath, lust burned.

He'd felt that energy the second he'd walked into the stall. He'd heard it in the pattern of her breathing. A week ago he would have attributed the undercurrent of tension to anger. Today, in the quiet confines of Dottie's stall, he'd recognized it for what it was—suppressed desire. She wanted him, and she was fighting it for all she was worth.

The man he used to be would have capitalized on the situation. He could have made love to her today. She was ripe for it. One touch would have tipped the balance in his favor, and the sex would have been glorious. She would have temporarily reveled in the unexpected encounter, the thrill of tasting forbidden fruit.

But afterward…ah, that was the problem. She would be ashamed of herself for surrendering to urges that vi-

olated her principles. Pleasure would quickly become
tainted. And then, if the sex had been so good that
she *still* wanted him, despite everything, she'd begin
to hate herself and him. He knew all about that downward spiral. He'd put Jeannette through it. He'd put
himself through it.

As he pulled up in front of the little cabin he temporarily called home, he vowed that he would not subject
Tracy to the same fate as Jeannette. If that meant they'd
never explore the possibilities presented by their strong
chemistry…oh, well.

He'd been celibate for months, and he was almost
getting used to it. He and Jeannette had tried to create a
relationship after Regan had left, tried to convince each
other that their betrayal of Regan had been motivated by
a grand passion they couldn't deny. The fantasy hadn't
held up for very long, and since breaking off with Jeannette, he hadn't felt like getting involved with anyone.

Parking his dusty black SUV, he went inside the
cabin and turned on his laptop. He ordered the supplements to be shipped to the rescue facility and texted instructions to Tracy's cell so she'd know how and when
to administer them. And that, he thought, should be
the end of that.

He could have done more. A rectal and vaginal exam
would have been normal procedure, but the mare appeared healthy and Regan would be back in charge in a
week. Drake had enjoyed the chance to be a vet again,
even briefly, and that surprised him. Lately he'd wondered if he needed to change careers as well as his place
of residence, but maybe not.

Considering the delicate situation with Tracy, though, he would perform only basic care unless a problem cropped up. Tracy was a smart lady. If she needed help, she'd call. If she didn't, then they could avoid contact with each other, contact that might lead to actions they'd both regret.

As he decided whether to go on a hike or read a book, neither of which appealed to him, someone knocked on his front door. Although he was glad for an interruption in what promised to be a boring afternoon, he couldn't imagine who had come to visit. No one sought him out besides Regan, and he was in Washington.

Drake opened the door and discovered Josie Chance there. He tried not to look as astonished as he felt. Thanks to Regan making a few introductions after he and Drake had rescued their friendship, Drake recognized the attractive woman wearing her long blond hair in a braid down her back.

A few years ago she'd married Jack Chance, the oldest of the Chance brothers and their avowed leader. But that wasn't the most significant fact about Josie Chance. She happened to own the Spirits and Spurs, which made her Tracy's boss. Drake suspected that Tracy was the reason behind Josie's visit.

Josie didn't disappoint him. "This isn't exactly a social call, Drake. I'm here to talk about Tracy."

"Be glad to." He wasn't, but he'd been raised to say the polite thing. "Come on in."

She walked through the door and glanced around the small space furnished with a sturdy sofa and chair covered in green plaid. "Very nice."

"Yes, ma'am." He wasn't sure what she meant, but agreeing with her seemed like a good strategy.

She gave him a small, almost reluctant smile. "I wasn't sure if you'd be a typical bachelor living in chaos."

"Because that's what scoundrels do?"

Her smile widened. "Often, yes."

"I did live in chaos for a little while, but when the maid didn't show up I decided I might as well keep it clean myself before I started losing things in the mess I'd made. Please, have a seat. I can brew some coffee, and I also have iced tea in the refrigerator."

"Sweet tea?"

"No, ma'am. I know it's not very Southern of me, but I like mine plain."

"I'll have some, then. Thank you." She sat in the easy chair. "Tracy would kill me if she knew I'd come over here."

Drake took a couple of tall glasses out of the cupboard and filled them with ice. "I won't tell her, but good luck keeping a secret around here."

"You're right, but I'm going to attempt it. Jack's the only one who knows I rode over, because I needed someone who could watch little Archie without throwing a hissy-fit about me coming. Three of my potential babysitters are Regan's sisters, and they would *not* approve."

"I'm sure." He poured tea in both glasses. "Wait a minute. You *rode* over here from the Last Chance?"

"It's closer to go cross-country, and doing that made it less likely I'd be seen. My horse is out back, tied to a tree."

"I'll be damned." He walked over and handed her one of the glasses before sitting on the sofa with his own drink. "You've infiltrated enemy territory."

"Something like that." She took a swallow of her tea. "This is excellent. Thanks."

"It's one of the few things I know how to make." He settled back, his glass balanced on one knee. "So you're here on a secret mission to make sure the big bad wolf doesn't have designs on the fair maiden Tracy?"

"That about sums it up." She studied him. "You're charming. I assumed you would be."

"Back in Virginia, it's the law. Anyone who fails the Southern-charm test is shipped up north."

"Oh, boy." Josie sipped her tea. "This could be trickier than I thought."

"It won't be tricky." Drake met her gaze. "I've already thought this through. I'll admit that I find Tracy very attractive, but I—"

"I *knew* it. Unfortunately, she's fascinated with you, too. You should hear the way she carries on about your dastardly behavior, to the point where I finally realized she was into you."

If having that confirmed thrilled him, he didn't want to let on. "But she doesn't want to be."

"Exactly. Do you know why?"

"Sure. Like everyone else around here, she doesn't like what I did to Regan." He took a long pull on his iced tea and concentrated on the cool liquid running down his throat. God, but he was sick of this topic. Maybe someday in the distant future his indiscretions wouldn't be the main thing folks wanted to talk to him about.

"It goes deeper than that, and I decided it might help if you understood a little more about her."

Now this he did want to hear. "Shoot."

"Her father was a married man who claimed he was single and that he'd had a vasectomy."

"Oh." At one time Drake would have offered a comment on that kind of behavior, but he no longer felt qualified to pass judgment.

"That's why infidelity is such a complicated issue for Tracy. She hates it, but without it she wouldn't exist. Her dad sent a few checks, but by then he was back with his wife. When the checks stopped coming, Tracy's mom didn't go after the bastard because she's not well educated and didn't think she could get anywhere, legally."

"Is Tracy's mother still around?"

"She eventually married some old cowboy from Idaho and she lives over there, now. But Tracy's roots are here, so she stayed. Most of us feel as if we helped raise her."

Drake nodded. "She probably feels that way, too." Setting his tea on the coffee table in front of him, he leaned back and blew out a breath. "I'm glad you told me all that, although I'd already decided after going over there today that I'd—"

"Going over there?" Josie straightened. "Was there a problem with the animals?"

"Not exactly." He gave her a brief rundown on what had happened with the pregnant Appaloosa.

"Okay. That's not so terrible. Regan and Lily will have a good time with a foal running around, and maybe they'll decide to hire this Rankin fellow. If not, Jack might have a spot for him at the Last Chance."

"His mare's in decent shape, so he's probably good with horses, but that's all I can vouch for."

"Jack can ask around about him. I just hope the mare will wait until Regan and Lily get back before she delivers."

"Me, too." He planned to be strong in the face of temptation, but he'd rather not be tempted by Tracy at all.

"You were saying something about a decision after going over there today. I didn't let you finish."

Drake wasn't sure he wanted to finish. They'd finally left the topic he was so sick of, and that was a relief. But he supposed he might as well say his piece. "I plan to keep my distance from Tracy. I already have one woman on my conscience who got involved with me against her better judgment. I don't need to make it two."

"You're talking about Regan's ex-fiancée."

"Yes, ma'am."

"For what it's worth, I don't believe in laying all the blame on you, but people are probably doing that because you're here. You're the sacrificial goat, the one who showed up to take the flak. I happen to think that half the responsibility is hers."

"I can't say that's true." Drake had gone over the night's events a million times, and he always saw himself as the one who could have stopped it. Should have stopped it.

"Noble of you. Egotistical, too, I might add."

He blinked. "Excuse me?"

"Do you really consider yourself so irresistible that a woman loses her ability to think for herself when you display your manly charms?"

He stared at her, and after the shock wore off, he started to laugh. Then he laughed until his sides hurt. Finally, he wiped his eyes and cleared his throat. "Thanks for that. You've lightened my load quite a bit."

She regarded him with amusement. "I wasn't prepared to like you very much, Drake. It's disconcerting to find out that I like you a lot."

"Good. I like you, too."

"The problem is, I'm not even supposed to be here, so I can't go around telling people that you're actually a pretty nice guy if they'd only get to know you."

He shrugged. "That's okay. Regan keeps telling me to give everyone time."

"Yeah, well, there are a few around here who are world-champion grudge holders, so don't expect a miracle. But now that you mention it, that's something I've been very curious about. What are your plans? Are you staying? Are you going back to Virginia? Regan's always been vague about your next move."

"That's because I'm vague about it. I don't want my old life back, but I'm not sure what my new life should look like, or where it will take place. I'm at a crossroads."

She studied him quietly for a moment. "There's this spot out on the ranch, a big flat piece of granite laced with quartz that's sacred to the Shoshone Indians, although they really don't go out there anymore. Some say that if you're having trouble deciding what to do, standing out on that rock helps."

"What do you think?"

"I've never personally used that rock to make a decision, but some of my loved ones have. It couldn't hurt."

"Oh, yes, ma'am, it could. I've heard that in the Wild West trespassers get shot at, especially if they're considered villainous cads, which I am."

Josie grinned. "I wish you and Jack could spend some time together without starting a family feud. I think you'd get along. Anyway, let me give you my cell number. If you decide to head out there, call me and I'll make sure the coast is clear."

"It's a deal."

When they were finished with their tea, they went out back to fetch Josie's horse.

Drake walked outside with her. "It was mighty kind of you to come by," he said.

"I mostly did it for Tracy." She untied her horse, a large bay, and put on the hat she'd hung from the saddle horn. "I hoped to appeal to your better instincts."

"You did, although I was already headed in that direction."

She mounted up and gazed down at him. "That's good to hear, Drake. I wish you well."

"Sounds as if I have one more friend around here."

"You do, but if you mess with Tracy, I'll quickly become Enemy Number One."

"I understand."

"Call if you want a spiritual boost from the sacred rock."

"I will."

With a wave, she guided her horse to the front of the cabin and rode off. Drake followed and watched her dismount to lower the rail on the wooden fence marking the edge of Last Chance property. Then she led her horse across, replaced the rail and climbed back into the saddle before cantering across the meadow.

It struck him that although he'd devoted his life to horses, he hadn't ridden much. His parents owned thoroughbreds destined for the track, and so did all his clients. He'd passed the weight limit for being a jockey when he was twelve, and besides, he'd never aspired to that career.

As a kid, he'd been given one of the thoroughbreds that balked at the starting gate. He'd ridden Black Velvet for a few years, but then school and girls had claimed most of his attention. His riding had become sporadic and mostly confined to summer vacations.

He couldn't remember the last time he'd ridden. He knew everything about the animal—skeletal structure, muscles, tendons, circulatory system…the list went on. But somewhere along the way he'd lost track of the riding part.

Back in Virginia he rented a town house. It had never really occurred to him to buy horse property. He could guess why. He had no desire to own a stable of racehorses, and that was the only model he'd known.

But there were other models. The Last Chance was one of them. Regan and Lily's equine-rescue facility was another. He'd allowed his view to become very narrow, but a relationship with horses didn't have to involve running them around a track or even caring for their medical needs.

He wouldn't mind taking a ride now, but he couldn't go over to the rescue facility and borrow a horse, and he wouldn't be welcome at the Last Chance, either. He could try to find a riding stable in the area, but he probably was too spoiled to be satisfied with most stable ponies.

Still, he'd had another epiphany. Whatever his future held, he wanted it to involve riding horses. Good thing he'd made some wise investments, because horse property didn't come cheap no matter where he ended up. He had a rough idea what his parents' farm was worth, and the amount was staggering.

Eventually he chose a hike over spending the rest of the day in the cabin reading. He took an easy trail, one he could manage in hiking sandals and shorts. The afternoon was warm, so he wore a sleeveless T-shirt. Exercise was a great stress reliever and helped keep his mind off Tracy and his pesky libido. He pocketed his phone out of habit, and he was on the trail headed home when her call came.

"Dottie is leaking," she said.

"Leaking what?" His heart pounded. He didn't want anything leaking. He didn't want anything going wrong with the mare—for several reasons.

"I think it's milk, or something like milk. What does that mean?"

"It means I need to come over and check her out. Unlock Regan's truck. I've been hiking, so I'm hot and sweaty. You'll have to take me the way I am."

"Don't worry about that." She sounded frightened. "Just get here."

"I will, and don't be scared. Everything will be fine." He didn't know that for sure, but it was a good thing to say when people were upset.

Although he didn't shower, he pulled on jeans, boots and a long-sleeved Western shirt before hopping in the SUV. Shorts and hiking sandals weren't the most practical thing to have on if he ended up delivering a foal. As he drove back to the rescue facility, he concentrated on his reasons for being there. This was all about the horse and her foal. Taking her in had been an act of mercy that could end up with everyone feeling warm and fuzzy, unless something went wrong.

If she was lactating, that was a sign that she was closer to giving birth than he'd thought. But the colostrum she'd produce at first was critical to the health of the foal and should be collected. Lactating early could also be a sign of serious trouble that could lead to fatalities, both the mare's and the foal's. He didn't plan to let tragedy occur.

Tracy was standing in the yard, arms wrapped around her torso, when he drove through the gate she'd obviously left open for him. As he turned off the engine and climbed out, she hurried over, all hesitation swept away by panic. He was tempted to gather her in his arms to comfort her, but that wasn't a good idea, and it wasn't what she needed from him right now.

"It's not just the leaking," she said. "It's her whole behavior. She's pacing the stall. Sometimes she lies down, but then she gets up again. I drove Regan's truck down to the barn so you'll have whatever you need close by."

"Thanks. Good idea. Let's go see what our girl is up to." He walked fast, Tracy skipping to keep up with him. Before this, she'd always maintained a certain physical distance between them, but that didn't seem important to her anymore.

"Maybe I shouldn't have taken her, but I don't know what Jerry would have done if I hadn't. If she needs veterinary care, he wouldn't have been able to afford that, either. I'm so glad you're here, Drake."

His heart stuttered. He hadn't realized how much he'd longed for someone—*anyone*—to say that to him. After being persona non grata for so long, those words sounded damned good.

She rattled on, obviously needing to vent. "I did some research online and found out she should have a bigger stall, but the stalls are all the same size. Do you think she'll be okay in there? The way she's been pacing, I thought maybe she needed more room, but I don't know what we can do about that."

"The one she's in will be fine. All the stalls in this barn are a generous size." He was touched by her anxiety. At Spirits and Spurs she was in complete control as she dispensed food and drink with flair. But now she was in unfamiliar territory. Fortunately it was familiar to him.

The July sun was drifting slowly toward the horizon, but it wouldn't be dark for another couple of hours. The barn faced east and west, and she'd opened the back doors to let in the afternoon light. Drake was happy to have the sun. A crisis always loomed larger in the dark.

Sure enough, Dottie was pacing restlessly in her stall and ignoring her flake of hay while the other horses munched their dinner contentedly. Drake talked calmly to her as he entered and kept talking as he ran his hands over her warm coat. Gradually he made his way to her udder and swiped a finger over the liquid oozing from her teat. Apparently he'd misjudged how soon she'd deliver.

Tracy hovered at his elbow, her breathing shallow. "Well?"

He turned to look at her. Her face was pale with fright, and this close, he noticed little flecks of gold in her dark eyes. "The discharge is colostrum, which is extremely important for her foal's immune system. It's good that you noticed. I'll get what I need from Regan's truck so we can collect and freeze it until she goes into labor. Then we can bottle feed it to her foal in the first twelve hours."

Her eyes widened. "When do you think she'll go into labor?"

"Could be anytime, and I can teach you how to—"

"Did you say *anytime?*"

"Yes, but I can't say for sure exactly when. Could be tonight, could be tomorrow, could be two days from now. In the meantime, you can—"

"Look, I hate to ask this of you, but I'm scared to death. I won't have the faintest idea what to do if she goes into labor, and I could freak. I'm freaked now, in fact. She's not safe with me."

He had to admit she looked petrified, but he could talk her down. She could do this. "She's perfectly safe with you, Tracy. I'm not far away, and all you have to do is call me. I'll be here before you know it."

She shook her head. "Not good enough. I can feed the animals, clean up after them and love on them, but I'm not fit to be a first responder when a mare delivers a foal. Besides, I have to work my shifts at the Spirits and Spurs, and Dottie would be alone for hours. That could be a problem, right?"

He'd forgotten about that. "Do you have to work tonight?"

"No, but I have to go in at eleven tomorrow morning. What if she waits to go into labor until then?"

"You can call me." But he was less sure that everything would work out easily. Dottie had changed the game considerably in the past couple of hours.

"Drake, if you leave, I'll spend the night camped out next to her stall worried sick with my phone right next to me."

He believed her. "Then *I'll* camp out beside her stall tonight. I'm sure there are some old blankets in the house I can use to make a bedroll."

"You don't have to go *that* far. Lily has a spare room. You could sleep in there, maybe set your phone to wake you up every few hours to check on her and collect that stuff the foal will need."

"Colostrum."

"Right. Colostrum."

He hesitated. Sleeping in the barn was one thing.

Sleeping in the house with Tracy was a whole other deal. "That's okay. The barn's fine."

"No, no, just because I said I would sleep there if you left doesn't mean you should put yourself through that. You're a pro. You'll know whether it's safe to grab a few winks, and you'd be better off in a real bed."

"Yeah, but—"

"I'll bet you don't want to stay in the house because you think I don't like you."

"You don't like me." *But once your panic wears off, you'll be attracted to me, whether you want to be or not.*

"I don't like what you did to Regan, and I don't blame you for not wanting to hang around someone who's said some hurtful things, but I'm desperate. Please stay. And take the guest room."

He took a deep breath. "Okay." Once the crisis was over, they'd both be like dry kindling ready to ignite. He'd have to get the hell out of there before one of them lit the fire.

4

ON SOME LEVEL, Tracy knew she was taking a huge chance by having Drake close by, but she simply couldn't handle this alone. She walked out to the truck with him. "Since you're staying, I'll share the money Regan and Lily pay me for house-sitting."

"I wouldn't consider it." He opened the back end of the truck. "You need that money for school."

"I do, but if you're doing part of my job here, then it's only fair that...wait a minute. How did you know I'm going to school?"

He gave her a deer-in-the-lights look followed by an expression that clearly said *oh, shit*. He tried to pass it off with a shrug. "That's the way it is around here with secrets. Word gets out."

"Sure it does, but not to you. You don't talk to anybody except Regan and Lily. At least not about anything significant. One of them told you, didn't they?"

"Regan told me and then asked me not to mention it, which I just did. Blame it on my big mouth instead of

Regan blabbing. He was trying to respect your privacy, but he thought I might want to know."

"Why?"

"He thought…" A dull red colored his throat and moved up to his cheeks. "Never mind. It's not important." He leaned into the truck and began sorting through Regan's supplies.

"Okay." She was ready to let the subject drop, at least for now. Apparently her previous high anxiety had blocked her sexual awareness of Drake, because as it fell, her heat level rose. And here she was, within the three-foot limit, which hadn't been a problem when she was hyperventilating over the possibility she'd have to deliver a foal.

Now it was a problem, especially with him leaning over like that, which showcased his tight buns. She backed away from the truck. "I need to feed the pigs and chickens. When I discovered Dottie leaking, I lost track of everything else."

"Sure. Go ahead." Rustling noises indicated he was still gathering supplies. He didn't turn around. "I'll take care of things here."

Then she realized something else. She should offer to feed *him*—another sticky wicket because logically they'd have to eat the meal together. He might have to spend considerable time within her three-foot limit. Maybe they could sit at opposite ends of Lily and Regan's dining table as if they were a couple living in a manor house with servants.

Then there was the menu. She doubted it would suit him, but she had to give it a shot. She'd talked him into occupying the premises, and the guy needed nourishment. A small town like Shoshone didn't have a pizza parlor that delivered.

She screwed up her courage. "After I feed the pigs and chickens, I'll warm up some dinner for us."

He turned around, a box in one hand. "That would be great." He gave her a quick smile.

The effect was potent. She backed up another step. "I should warn you that Lily's a vegetarian and Regan's reverted to vegetarianism, too."

"I know. I've been over for dinner a few times."

"Right. I guess you would have." So maybe this food situation would work out okay, after all. "Anyway, she was nice enough to prepare and freeze some food for me. I've thawed a container of lentil soup for tonight. There's plenty for both of us, and she also made corn bread."

"I'm good with that."

She detected a distinct lack of enthusiasm, but she wasn't surprised. Not a lot of guys became excited over lentil soup. "There's also a huge chocolate cake."

"*Now* we're talkin'!"

She couldn't help laughing. "Do you want dessert first?"

"No, I do not. I'm not five. I'll eat my lentil soup like a good boy."

"All right." She did her best not to be charmed, but it was cute the way he drew out the word *five*.

"Besides, it's got to be better than the frozen dinners I've cooked for myself whenever I didn't come into town for a meal."

She had a sudden image of Drake alone in the small cabin eating a microwaved meal by himself and felt a twinge of sympathy. She had so many friends, while he… No, she would *not* feel sorry for him. He could always go back to Virginia and resume his old life. For whatever reason, he'd chosen to stay here and be lonely.

"I've had Lily's lentil soup," she said. "It's good. Come on up to the house when you're finished here." She turned and walked away. All the way to the house she lectured herself about not letting down her guard.

She knew all about the big flaw in Drake's character. That should have been enough to keep her far, far away from him. Her mother had been seduced by a charmer like Drake, but her mother hadn't had Tracy's advantage of knowing she was dealing with a cheating bastard.

Yes, he was coming to her aid at the moment, and she was thrilled about that. But she couldn't let gratitude and her natural susceptibility override her good judgment. Somehow she had to strike a balance between being properly appreciative and throwing herself into his arms in a fit of lust. She wondered if simple friendship was an option. That might be the safe middle ground, assuming she could pull it off.

Drake had betrayed his best friend, someone Tracy greatly admired. As she stood in the kitchen chopping veggies for the potbellied pigs, she faced a truth she'd been unwilling to admit until now. Drake was also extremely likable. Her choices would be so much easier if he could behave like an arrogant jerk. Then she'd have no trouble separating the guys in the white hats from the ones in the black hats.

She finished filling the bowls for Wilbur and Harley and carried them out to their pens. At one time the two pigs had been free to roam the yard, but the bigger one, Harley, had bullied Wilbur into giving up his food. Now they each had a separate pen for mealtimes, although both had a gate out to a common yard and mud hole they could enjoy together when they weren't eating.

Tracy set a bowl in each pen and then quickly closed them in their respective homes. "That's the answer." She leaned against the fence and watched the pigs eat. "I should be friendly, because after all, the guy is doing me a big-ass favor. But I need to set boundaries, just like you have these fences between you."

Having Drake sleep in the spare room would be no problem if they established some house rules. She couldn't appear inhospitable, because after all, she'd invited him to stay. Perhaps she'd even begged him. Her memory wasn't clear on that point because she'd been distraught at the time.

But now that he'd agreed, they needed to establish a routine that would minimize…temptation. No, she couldn't phrase it like that. The word *temptation* shouldn't come up. They would strive to minimize…unanticipated encounters. That sounded stuffy. She'd have to find a better description, but that's what she meant.

For example, he should keep his shirt on at all times. If he was in the habit of wandering into the kitchen for a midnight snack, he couldn't do that in his pajama bottoms. He had to put on… Uh-oh. He didn't *have* pajama bottoms.

She hadn't thought this through. She'd pleaded with

him to stay, but he hadn't come prepared with extra clothes or toiletries. He certainly hadn't come with pajamas, either tops or bottoms. Besides, he wouldn't want to sleep in them, anyway, if he planned to check on Dottie periodically.

She *really* hadn't thought about how this would work. But now she could see it all playing out in living color. He'd sleep in his briefs, unless he chose to sleep naked. When he got up to check on the mare, he'd put on the basics—jeans, socks, boots. It was mid-July. Bothering with a shirt under the circumstances would be plain silly.

Well, then, she'd stay in her room. That would solve the problem. No, it wouldn't. She definitely wanted to be in on the action when Dottie gave birth. She couldn't picture herself cowering in her room like some nervous virgin because Drake was shirtless while he delivered a foal. That would be stupid.

"Still feeding the pigs?" The man in question walked toward her with a loose-hipped stride and a casual smile. He was sexy as hell.

"I'm just finishing up." He'd look amazing without his shirt. Tracy had no doubt about that. If only he could have a potbelly like the pigs, but then he wouldn't have been able to seduce Regan's fiancée, which was the crux of the problem.

She had no idea how she'd handle the temptation of a bare-chested Drake, especially in the likely event that Dottie delivered her foal in the middle of the night. Tracy vaguely remembered discussions among the cowboys at Spirits and Spurs that mares often gave birth at night.

"I didn't realize you'd be so fast." She pushed away from the fence as he moved past the five-foot mark and the tingle of awareness began traveling through her body.

"Dottie's colostrum production is still fairly minimal, which is good. The less she produces before giving birth, the better."

Three feet. Her skin began to warm. "I haven't started on dinner." She gestured toward the pigs. "I like to wait until they're done so I can let them back into their communal area. They love being together, except I can't allow it when they eat."

"Yeah, Lily explained that to me." Drake stood next to her and peered down at the two pigs. "Harley seems a little skinnier, though, so I guess the new program is working."

"It's working." And her libido was working, too. Overtime, in fact. Her hormones were racing around like a championship Roller Derby team.

He'd come here straight from hiking, something she remembered now. If the deodorant commercials were correct, his manly sweat should offend her. But something primitive was going on, because she longed to bury her nose in his shirt and take a big sniff of that heady scent. And then she'd...

"Look at that pig eat!" Drake sounded amused. "He's practically licking the bowl."

"Yeah. He's insatiable." Whoops. Not the best choice of words under the circumstances.

Drake's low chuckle held an undercurrent of awareness. "Hey, Harley, are you gonna let the lady talk about you like that?"

"Well, he is." As if she had no sense of self-preservation, she looked into Drake's laughing eyes. Oh, Lord. She glanced away, but not quickly enough to mute the effect. Every secret, private place in her body responded. "I can let them loose now." Her voice had a huskiness that she was very afraid he'd notice.

"You're sure that's a good idea? Lily used to let them roam the property, but from what I hear, that didn't work out well."

"I mean let them into their community area. They'll still be fenced in."

"Oh, right. Yeah, that's better."

As she walked over and opened the gates so they could both scurry into the communal pen, she told herself that she and Drake were having a conversation about the pigs. But if they had been, he should have been watching them. Instead his attention remained firmly on her, his gaze assessing.

After she let the pigs into their shared enclosure, she faced him. "I desperately need you to stay here tonight, and maybe for the next several nights."

He remained watchful. "I know, and I've agreed to do that. It makes sense."

"But asking you to stay doesn't mean that I—"

"Of course not." Pain was reflected ever so briefly in his expression. "I've been waiting for you to warn me off. Why would you get involved with a man you don't like very much?" Bitterness laced his comment.

In a flash of insight, she knew that he'd picked up on her unbidden reaction to him. Knowing she wanted him even though she didn't approve of him was…insulting? Degrading? Maybe both. "Drake, I—"

"No worries." His jaw tightened. "I wouldn't dream of causing you to do something you don't want to do. Women tend to have a certain response to me. Always have, ever since I was a teenager. Mostly it's fun for both parties, but in this case…"

She'd hurt his feelings. There was no way around it. "I'm sorry."

"Just for the record, I don't make a habit of moving in on another man's territory." He massaged the back of his neck and glanced away. "I've only done it once, and if I could take it back, I would." Then he sighed and looked over at her. "I've never said that to anybody. It sounds like doing it once is no big deal when I know it is. I just wish… Damn it, I wish that one stupid mistake wasn't the only thing you saw when you looked at me."

At that moment, it wasn't the only thing she saw. She saw a man who, for whatever reason, had betrayed himself as well as his best friend. She believed him when he claimed never to have cheated before or since. But why had it happened at all? She thought the answer would be complicated, and unraveling complicated motivations was her passion.

He gave her a crooked smile. "You have that look on your face again."

"What look?"

"The same one you got back at the Spirits and Spurs when I said I must be a glutton for punishment. I told

Regan about your reaction, and that's when he mentioned your field of study."

"Huh." She wasn't sure which surprised her more—that he'd been paying such close attention to her expressions or that he and Regan had been discussing her that night and she'd had no idea. Apparently she'd been so wrapped up in being cool that she'd missed some things.

"I figure, when you look like that, you're fixin' to psychoanalyze me."

"And you wouldn't like that."

"Not much, mostly because you've already decided I'm a bad character. I don't think your evaluation would be unbiased."

She flushed at that truth. "You're right. It's a failing of mine. Being judgmental is a no-no for a psychologist, and I *am* judgmental. I'll have to give that up if I expect to be an effective therapist."

"Then why not start with me?"

"I thought you didn't want me to work with you."

"I don't if you consider me lower than whale poop."

"I don't consider you lower than whale poop." That was hard to say without laughing. "Whale poop is at the bottom of the ocean. That's as low as anybody can go, and I don't consider you that bad."

"Okay, then where would you rank me? How about lower than a snake's belly?"

She couldn't hold back a grin. "Stop it. You're being ridiculous."

"No, I'm not. I'm trying to get a bead on just how bad your bad opinion of me is."

"No, you're trying to charm me."

His expression was priceless, exactly like a kid caught with his hand in the cookie jar. "Busted." He gazed at her. "Was it working?"

"You know it was. It's what you do best. That's why I'm so leery of you."

"Leery? You mean like afraid?"

She thought about that. "Maybe."

"Why would you be afraid of me?" He spread his arms wide. "I'm completely harmless." Then he sniffed and made a face. "However, I stink to high heaven. I could use a shower before we sit down to eat. I can't stand myself, so I can only imagine what I'm puttin' you through. If you want to be judgmental about that, I wouldn't blame you a bit."

Smiling, she shook her head. "You just can't help it, can you?"

"Help what?"

"Never mind. Let's go back to the house so I can fix us some dinner and you can shower." She started walking in that direction, but her thoughts remained with their conversation. If she understood him correctly, he was offering himself as a guinea pig, but only if she could stop judging him long enough to help him work through some issues.

He fell into step beside her. "Obviously I didn't bring any spare clothes."

"I thought of that." She didn't want him to know how long she'd obsessed about it. "How close are you to Regan's size?"

"Pretty close, if you're willing to raid his underwear

drawer and maybe snag me a shirt or two. The jeans will be okay for another day or so."

"I'll see what I can find and leave them in your room."

"That would be great. While you're at it, maybe if you nose around you'll come up with a spare razor, and maybe even a new toothbrush and toothpaste. Regan typically has backup stuff like that. He likes being organized."

"I'll look. Under the circumstances, I'm sure he wouldn't care if I raid his bathroom supplies."

"If you'd rather not, I could make a quick run home. Maybe that would be better."

"No." Just the thought of him leaving caused panic to well up again. Her sense of security depended on him being right here. "Please don't."

"Okay, okay. I won't leave until Dottie drops her foal."

"Thank you." Her panic disappeared immediately. But now that they'd mentioned Dottie, she wanted to reassure herself that the mare was okay. "Let's check on her before we go in."

He nodded and switched direction. "Okay, assuming you can stand being around me for another ten minutes. If you want to let me do it while you head for the house, I won't be offended."

"I'll come with you." She adjusted her path, too. "It's good practice for me."

"Practice?"

"For learning to be less judgmental."

"Ah." He laughed and glanced over at her. "How

about it, Tracy? Any chance your practice could extend beyond putting up with my stench?"

"Such as what?" She had a pretty good idea what he was talking about, but she wanted to be sure.

"Would you be willing to practice accepting my considerable failings, too?"

She met his gaze. "I guess it's worth a shot."

"Good deal." He flashed his superwattage smile.

He might think he'd convinced her just now. In reality, he'd had her at whale poop.

5

DOTTIE HAD TEMPORARILY stopped leaking colostrum, so in short order Drake was back in the house and standing under a hot shower. He soaped up, grateful for the opportunity to get clean again. Tracy had found him a razor and a toothbrush. She'd even discovered an unused deodorant stick and a new tube of toothpaste that happened to be his brand. He'd replace all the items once this gig was over.

God, he hoped he knew what he was doing by agreeing to let Tracy muck around in his psyche. But he'd learned that solitary self-exploration didn't work for him, and he couldn't hang out in the little cabin forever waiting for enlightenment to arrive. He wanted a plan, but so far nothing had occurred to him.

As he'd predicted, his parents were royally pissed that he'd left in the middle of racing season. The guy who'd taken over his practice was quickly winning everyone's confidence, which irritated his parents even more. They'd shoveled clients his way for years, and now some other vet was reaping the rewards.

Drake didn't care. He might continue to be a vet, but not in the world of thoroughbred racing. He hoped his temporary replacement would be interested in buying him out, which would probably be the last straw for his folks. Oh, well. He'd tried it their way and had ended up so confused and miserable that he'd thought boinking his best friend's fiancée was a good idea.

Talking it out with Tracy would be a relief, providing she could give up her tendency to judge him. She'd admitted that was a problem area for her, so their cooperative effort might turn out to be a very good thing. Ideally, they'd help each other.

He hadn't decided what to do about sex. They both wanted to have it, but that didn't mean that they should. He'd pretty much promised Josie Chance that he wouldn't, and in a town like Shoshone there was zero probability that it would stay a secret.

For the moment he wouldn't worry about it. As he toweled off, he caught the subtle aroma of lentil soup warming on the stove. She must have put the corn bread in the oven as well, because he could smell that, too.

For the first time in months, he felt relaxed and almost peaceful. Tracy knew the worst about him, and yet she was fixing him supper. Better yet, she needed him around because of Dottie. Remembering her panic whenever she thought he might leave made him feel a little bit like her knight in shining armor. His armor might be tarnished, but she'd agreed to look past that for the time being.

By the time he walked into the kitchen wearing some of Regan's clothes but his own jeans and boots, she was in the dining room setting the table. She glanced up and smiled. "Dinner's almost ready, but I was wondering if you'd—"

"Take another look at Dottie?"

"Yeah. Am I being obsessive?"

"Nope." Even if he thought so, he wouldn't have said it. She'd taken on the responsibility of this pregnant mare, and she wouldn't rest easy until the foal had been born and both mother and baby were fine.

He wouldn't totally relax until that moment, either. Although he'd been through a lot of deliveries in his Virginia practice, most involving very valuable foals, this one loomed larger than all the others. He wanted to be Tracy's hero.

Walking outside, he took a deep breath of the warm evening air. The sun had disappeared moments ago, leaving an apricot glow behind. Enough light remained to make out the barn, which was pink with turquoise trim, and the house, painted neon green with orange trim. The orange almost matched the horizon.

Drake remembered his initial impression of this place, the day he and Regan had talked for the first time since the Christmas Eve incident. Regan had cautioned Drake not to make fun of the paint job. Lily was a free spirit who believed in shaking things up. Since that day, Drake had spent enough time here to grow used to the unusual colors, but newcomers always gawked and some of the old-timers muttered about the neighborhood going to hippie hell.

Drake had loyally defended Lily's paint choices to anyone who had criticized them in his presence. Considering his poor reputation around town, he'd wondered lately if maybe his defense had hurt more than helped her cause. So he'd become less vocal about it.

But the pink-and-turquoise barn appealed to him. The colors flew in the face of tradition, and he was all about that these days. His family was steeped in tradition. He might even say mired in it.

As he walked down to the barn, he realized that this equine-rescue facility made him happy. He'd forced himself not to come here too often because he hadn't wanted to be a pest, but now he had a perfect excuse to hang around and absorb the ambiance of this little five-acre piece of goodness and light.

He envied Regan, who planned to live here for the foreseeable future. He'd continue his vet practice with Nick Chance, and he'd provide free vet care for the animals that Lily took in. Sweet. Regan had found what he wanted in life. Drake was still searching for that perfect fit.

Inside the barn, he hit the switch that turned on some lights installed along the aisle near the floor. Regan said he'd patterned the lighting after what he'd seen in the much bigger barn at the Last Chance Ranch. Drake would have to take Regan's word for it. An invitation to the Last Chance, other than Josie's urging him to go stand on some sacred rock, didn't seem to be in his immediate future.

Familiar aromas greeted him as he walked down the wooden aisle—sweet hay, sun-dried straw, oiled leather and the earthy scent of horses. Would he like to own a barn like this someday? He might, if the horses weren't racing stock being groomed for the track. The intense focus of their lives had too closely mirrored his own, and the pressure had threatened to choke the breath out of him. At the time he hadn't recognized that.

When he came to Dottie's stall, she was quietly munching on the flake of hay she hadn't cared about earlier. She paid little attention to him as he walked into the stall. When he checked her teats, they were dry.

"Okay, pretty girl, what's the story?"

Dottie continued to ignore him as she ate her dinner.

"I hope you realize what a commotion you caused around here. You scared poor Tracy to death. So now what? Are you gonna make us all wait a week? Two weeks?"

The mare lifted her head long enough to gaze at him. But those liquid brown eyes gave nothing away. Then she went back to her meal.

"A lady of mystery, huh? Okay. I'll go eat my dinner and be back later. I don't quite trust this lull in the action. I think you have more tricks up your sleeve."

Giving Dottie a final pat on the rump, he walked out of the stall and latched it behind him. He could take a blood sample, but in the end it was still a guessing game. If Regan were here, he'd use his intuitive skills and probably pinpoint the moment of birth within a few minutes. That was why he was a great vet and Drake was merely an adequate one.

But he'd bring his A-game to this event. Lacking Regan's horse-whisperer instincts, he'd set his phone alarm to ring on the hour every hour until dawn. If he lost a little sleep, it didn't matter. He was no longer on a rigid schedule.

Tracy had turned on some lights in the house, and the cozy look of it beckoned to him. Funny how much he felt at home, even though both he and Tracy were visitors here. A week from now, regardless of what happened with Dottie, he and Tracy would be gone. Yet at this moment, he felt grounded, as if he finally belonged somewhere. Weird.

When he opened the screen door and walked inside, he had the insane urge to call out *Honey, I'm home!* He didn't, both because it would be lame and because she might think he'd gone completely nuts. She was studying psychology, which logically had to include abnormal psych. He didn't want to be classified with that second bunch.

Even so, he should at least announce his presence, in case she hadn't heard him come in. He didn't want to startle her. "Hey, Tracy!" he called out. "I'm back!"

"Good." Her voice came from the kitchen. "I'll take the corn bread out now."

Damn, but this was homey. He'd deliberately avoided sharing a condo or apartment with a woman because he'd known he wasn't even close to settling down. The thought had always felt stifling. Yet this...was not.

Tracy was in the process of setting the corn-bread pan on the stove when he walked into the kitchen. She glanced over at him, her face flushed with the heat from cooking. Her ponytail was coming loose, and little wisps of dark hair at her nape were damp with sweat. "How's Dottie?"

He longed to get her even hotter and sweatier. It would be so simple to walk over there and gather her into his arms. He couldn't be absolutely sure how she'd react, but he didn't think she'd resist once she got over the initial surprise. Women seemed to like the way he kissed.

She probably thought of him as some sort of Don Juan, though. She eventually might forgive his betrayal of Regan, but he couldn't deny that he was popular with the ladies. At least he had been before coming here. If he and Tracy ended up having sex, it would be a hundred times better if she made the first move.

So instead of crossing the room and kissing her, he stayed where he was and answered her question. "Honestly? If I didn't know better, I'd say that mare's decided not to deliver for a couple of weeks. Her teats are perfectly dry now." He walked over to the sink and started washing up.

"So it's a false alarm." She picked up a knife and cut the corn bread into squares. "I brought you out here for nothing."

"Not at all." And even if Dottie had issued a false alarm, he'd never think this trip was for nothing. He loved being here with Tracy. It was the most fun he'd had since arriving in Jackson Hole. "Something's going on, or she wouldn't have produced that colostrum this afternoon. I still plan to watch her closely tonight."

As she transferred pieces of corn bread into a napkin-draped basket, she paused to look at him. "You'll come and get me if she goes into labor, right?"

"You bet." He was counting on the excitement of the moment to distract him from the temptation she'd present when she was half-awake and wearing something skimpy. "You wouldn't want to miss the main event."

"Absolutely not." She held out the basket of corn bread. "You can take this into the dining room and I'll bring the soup. Oh, I nearly forgot. There's wine. Do you want any? Or a beer?"

He shook his head. He didn't need a fuzzy brain, both because of the mare and because of the hot woman he was determined not to touch until she touched him. "We can save that for a celebration after the foal is born." He wondered if that would be when Tracy let down her hair and her barriers. Maybe. He hoped Dottie would give birth real soon.

"Good idea. I won't have any, either. We should stay sharp. I'll bring us some water."

Drake had to smile as he walked into the dining room. She'd lit the tapers sitting in silver holders in the center of the table. Regan had given Lily those candlesticks, and since then the happy couple had eaten by candlelight almost every evening. Drake was touched that Tracy thought he was worthy of candles.

Place mats had been put down, too, he noticed, and cloth napkins. A plate to hold the soup bowl stood waiting at each place. A butter dish was already on the table. "This looks nice." He positioned the basket of corn bread where they both could reach it.

"I don't entertain often." She walked in with a bowl

of steaming soup in each hand and placed them on the table. "Lily and Regan are set up for it, and I decided to make things festive as a way to thank you for donating your time to this effort."

"It's my pleasure." It was the polite thing to say, but the words had never been truer.

"Choose your seat."

He glanced at the table. She'd arranged the place settings so that one of them would be at the head of the table and the other to that person's right. He stood behind the chair at the second spot. "I'll sit here."

She laughed. "I figured you for the head of the table."

"Why?"

"I don't know. You sound like Rhett Butler, and he would take the head of the table."

"I'm happy to destroy another stereotype."

"Then have a seat."

"Not yet. I might not automatically sit at the head of the table, but I'm Southern to the bone, which means I will help you into your chair."

"Oh!" She smiled brightly. "That would be lovely." She paused until he came around. "Sarah Chance would approve of your manners."

"Is that right?" He pulled out Tracy's chair, waited until she was seated, and slid the chair smoothly up to the table, just as he'd been taught as a boy. This close, he was tempted to lean down and kiss the soft skin behind her ear, but she'd probably jump ten feet if he did. Releasing his hold on her chair, he moved to his own and sat down.

Tracy put her napkin in her lap. "Sarah's big on manners, including the old-fashioned things like holding a lady's chair and opening doors. All three of her sons are known for it. The cowhands who work for her are expected to behave that way, too."

"Is she Southern?" He'd pretty much given up on the idea of making friends with Sarah, the matriarch at the Last Chance Ranch. He hadn't met her, but she was reputed to be extremely protective of her extended family, which included Regan. She might approve of Drake's manners, but she certainly wouldn't approve of him.

"No, she was a Yankee originally. She's almost like the queen of this area."

"So I've heard." He understood why Regan hadn't taken him out to the ranch to meet Sarah. He kept hearing about the woman, though, and he couldn't shake the idea that if he had Sarah on his side, everyone else would ease up. He'd had a nice talk with Josie today. Maybe that was a start.

"I've known Sarah forever, so she doesn't intimidate me, but I can understand how she would affect others. She has a regal bearing about her, which makes sense if you know that her mother was a model and probably trained Sarah to have great posture, too."

"Guess so." He spread his napkin over his lap. "Thanks for feeding me."

"You're welcome, but Lily deserves the credit. I don't like to cook, so she made a special effort to leave food for me. Even though it's vegetarian, which I don't normally eat, Lily makes it really taste good. But you know that already because you've had dinner here before." She grabbed her spoon. "And I'm babbling. Sorry."

He had to agree that she *was* babbling, and her breathing was quick and shallow, too. When she looked at him, she never quite met his gaze, and her color was high. Interesting. Was she nervous about serving him a meal? He didn't think so. She'd served him a ton of meals at Spirits and Spurs. Then he thought of another potential reason for her behavior, and his pulse rate climbed.

She scooped up a spoonful of soup and immediately spit it back out. "Hot, hot!" She gulped some water. "Don't try it yet. Let it cool."

"Tracy? Are you okay?"

"Sure." She drank more water. "Just burned my tongue. Should've waited. Silly of me. I'm the one who heated it up, so I should have realized that it was—"

"You're babbling again."

"I am." She kept her gaze on her soup. Her cheeks turned even pinker.

"Why?"

"You…um…affect me when you're this close, especially if I don't have something else to think about, like pregnant mares and such." Her attention remained on her soup. "I tried to convince myself I could handle it fine, but…apparently not. I'm sorry. I mean, we should be able to enjoy a nice meal, but then you helped me into my chair, and I… This is ridiculous."

His heart beat faster and heat surged through his body to settle in his groin. Finally she was ready to admit she craved him as much as he craved her. Hallelujah. "What do you want me to do?" He knew what *he* wanted to do, but she had to make the call.

"Nothing. I don't know what's wrong with me. No guy has ever affected me this way. Just give me a minute."

That threw a bucket of ice water on his libido. In spite of their recent conversation, she still seemed to think wanting him was wrong. He pushed back from the table. "I wouldn't want to make you uncomfortable. I'll take a walk down to the barn. I have my phone. When you're finished eating, text me and I'll come back and have some dinner."

"Wait!"

He heard her chair scrape the floor, knew she'd left the table, but he kept walking. She felt desire for him but wanted nothing from him. He could take a hint. A two-by-four upside the head would be more subtle.

"Drake, I'm sorry!" Her footsteps sounded behind him. "It's just that—"

"You're not ready to trust me?" He turned when he reached the door. She was standing about five feet away, breathing hard. "Is that what you're trying to say, Tracy? Because that's what I'm hearing, and if that's the way you feel, then I'll make sure to keep my distance."

"That's not it!"

"I think it is. Text me when you've finished eating. I promise to stick around until Dottie has her foal, so don't worry about that. This is a big place. We can avoid each other." He walked out the door.

Damn it. Damn it to hell. He'd thought maybe he'd found someone who could help him shed the guilt he'd been carrying around for six months. Instead she'd only made things worse.

6

WELL, SHE'D CERTAINLY loused that up. Tracy stared at the screen door as Drake's words played in a continuous loop in her head. *You're not ready to trust me.*

No one could blame him for coming to that soul-shattering conclusion. She'd admitted to wanting him desperately, and when he'd been ready to do something about it, she'd told him not to. She'd implied that given time, she'd rather squelch this unwelcome lust. No wonder he'd left.

Now she had a decision to make. If she really was scared to death of getting involved with him, all she had to do was leave things as they were. He'd keep far away from her now that she'd thoroughly insulted him and stomped all over his pride.

She paced the living room as she tried to sort through her thoughts. An armed truce sounded awful. Peaceful Kingdom was a happy place, and although she wasn't as into the woo-woo stuff as Lily, she hated to pollute the environment with bad feelings.

Besides, she had a mare in the barn who was about to give birth. If she and Drake were barely speaking, the atmosphere during delivery would be strained. That couldn't be good for any of them.

Something should be done, and she had to do it. She might not be able to repair the damage, but she had to try. That required working through what had happened at dinner so she could explain it to Drake.

She resumed her seat at the table. Maybe revisiting the scene of the crime would help her think. Chewing was supposed to stimulate the brain, so she picked up a piece of corn bread and took a bite.

Obviously she'd responded in a knee-jerk fashion. Until he'd scooted her chair in, she'd managed to keep her sexual response at the level of a low hum. But then he'd come close, very close, and the hum had turned into a rock concert.

When that powerful surge of desire caught her off guard, she'd gone into panic mode. That had resulted in the babbling, which of course he'd noticed. Normally she wasn't prone to it, and he'd been around her enough to know that. He'd asked a direct question, and she'd responded with the truth. So far, not so bad.

But then he'd done the right thing, the gentlemanly thing, and asked if he could help. He'd behaved in the most admirable way possible in such a situation. He hadn't pounced or leered, or any of a million obnoxious responses that other guys might have had to her confession. He'd quietly asked what she wanted him to do, implying that he was willing to do *just about anything*. How great was that?

She'd brushed him off. Why? Closing her eyes, she let her head drop back in despair. She'd brushed him off because she was a big, fat coward. She knew why, but that didn't help a whole lot. She'd still done damage to a well-meaning guy.

Ever since she'd hit puberty, her mother had warned her that wanting a man too much was dangerous. Following that advice, Tracy had made sure to date nice men who didn't particularly turn her on. She'd had a lukewarm physical relationship with two of them. Both men had moved on, which hadn't bothered her at all.

When Drake had first showed up at Spirits and Spurs, red hazard lights had flashed. The closer he'd come, the more she'd been convinced—this was the man her mother had warned her about. And a mother's warning, issued early and often, wasn't easily set aside.

Leaping up from the dinner table and hauling Drake into the bedroom would have felt reckless. It would have been the kind of impetuous behavior guaranteed to create the disaster her mother had predicted.

That was her reason for responding to Drake the way she had—not that she wasn't willing to trust him, but that she needed time to think about the implications first, to assess and to regroup.

Now she'd taken that time, and several things had come to mind. First of all, the man who'd wronged her mother, aka Tracy's father, had neglected to mention that he was married. Drake wasn't married. Not even close. No wives or fiancées waited in the wings, because Regan would have known about them and told her.

And Regan brought up the second point. Drake had

won Regan's seal of approval, even though Regan easily could have told her to stay away from Drake. He hadn't because, other than that one slip, Regan believed in the guy.

Last of all, the jerk who had inadvertently become Tracy's father had claimed to have had a vasectomy so he could have unprotected sex with Tracy's mother. Tracy couldn't imagine Drake lying under those circumstances.

Maybe that was the bottom line for Drake Brewster. He had made a mistake, which meant he was human. It was a dilly of a mistake, but he obviously regretted it deeply. Other than his one false move, which from all indications had been a spur-of-the-moment bad decision, Drake was an honest man.

He was also hot, and she might have blown her chance to find out just how hot. That gave her a selfish motive for fixing what she'd broken. It wouldn't be easy. If she managed to fix it, Drake could still break her heart, and because her feelings for him were intense, it would likely be a nasty break.

She picked up another piece of corn bread. Risking heartbreak was the kind of chance people had to take if they wanted to experience something besides lukewarm sex. Until meeting Drake, she'd wondered if lukewarm was all she was destined to feel.

He'd corrected that misunderstanding. Had he ever. But when given an opportunity to prove that she, too, could have a grand passion, she'd been afraid to let herself go. She was still afraid, but no longer quite so terrified as she had been after the holding-out-her-chair incident. She was nervously ready to suit up and get into the game.

First she needed to check on something, though. She'd already raided Regan's toiletries once, so maybe taking one other item wouldn't hurt. And she'd replace everything, of course. No doubt he'd taken a box to D.C., but Drake said Regan liked backup supplies, so logically another box should be tucked away somewhere.

She found the item in question under the sink. After opening the box, she carried it to the guest room and set it on the nightstand next to the queen-size bed. Looking at that bed and imagining what might take place there later gave her goose bumps. But she also had to be prepared for rejection. Drake had a perfect right to turn her down.

Back in the dining room, she wolfed down her soup, which was almost cool, before dumping Drake's soup back in the pot and turning it on low. Then she wrapped the remaining corn bread in foil and put it in the oven on warm.

The clock was ticking. He must be wondering when he'd get to eat, but she had more to do before texting him. She located a pen, paper and an envelope and brought them to the table. The note took her longer than she would have liked, but it had to set the tone. Licking the envelope was the worst part of the job. So far no one had come up with envelope-flap glue that didn't taste like motor oil laced with menthol.

She wrote his name on the outside of the envelope and propped it against his water glass. After dishing

his soup, she put the corn bread back on the table and
ducked into her bedroom. Finally she emerged in her
red silk bathrobe with her hair loose, and texted him
that she was finished eating.

Time to disappear. She made a beeline for the guest
room, barely making it before she heard his booted footsteps on the wooden porch. The screen door creaked
open. He must have been hungry.

She lay in his bed in the dark, because dark was
how he'd left the room. A light on in there might have
alerted him to a change in the situation. Sound carried
perfectly in the still house, which allowed her to hear
the chair scrape as he sat down at the table.

She held her breath. Paper ripped. He was reading
her note, which she remembered in vivid detail.

Dear Drake,
My reaction to you was motivated by fear. I was
taught from an early age not to trust men who
made me feel as you do, because they would ruin
my life. So I've dated only safe guys who didn't
arouse scary emotions. I realize now that's a cow-
ardly way to live.
I haven't treated you well. I'd like a chance to
do better, but if you still want to keep distance be-
tween us, I understand completely. Please let me
know if Dottie goes into labor. Sleep well.
Yours, Tracy

How she would have loved to watch his expression
as he'd read the note, but short of setting up a remote

video feed, that would have been impossible. Thinking of the elaborate spy system she would have set up if she'd had time, she started to giggle and had to use a pillow to muffle the sound.

By the time she settled down again, she could hear the rhythmic sound of his spoon dipping in and out of his soup bowl. That noise stopped and paper crinkled, as if he'd wadded up the note. Then it crinkled again, as if he might be smoothing it out. He sighed.

She'd wanted to give him time to think, time when she wasn't around, just as she'd had when he'd left for the barn. What if he decided she wasn't worth the trouble? Finding her in his bed would not be a pleasant surprise then, would it? He might order her out of his room. At least she'd brought the robe to put on in case that happened.

No matter where she was now or what his decision might be, they couldn't have avoided an awkward moment whenever they'd come face-to-face again. So she'd chosen to create a meeting that was shocking and quick. It might be painful, like ripping off a bandage, or bracing, like cannonballing into a cold swimming hole. Either way, it wouldn't be boring.

If he sent her away, that would be a reasonable payback for how she'd treated him. But because he was seeking forgiveness, she hoped he'd be in a forgiving mood, too. She'd know soon enough. She could hear him loading the dishwasher.

He took some time in the kitchen, which probably meant he was putting away the leftovers and wiping down the counters, exactly as she would have done. And all the while he had to be thinking.

When he left the kitchen, she expected to hear steps coming down the hall toward where she lay trembling, torn between excitement and anxiety. That didn't happen. He walked somewhere else, and she wasn't sure where until the screen door squeaked again. The ornery man was going back down to the barn!

She groaned in frustration. For all she knew he'd sleep down there. It was a warm night. There were saddle blankets he could use if necessary. Because he was an equine vet, he'd probably spent his share of nights in a barn.

After waiting another few minutes to see if he'd come back, she realized her plan wasn't going to work the way she'd envisioned it. So she'd have to come up with a new plan. He'd had his thinking time, and now it was action time. She could still take him by surprise.

A few minutes later she headed out to the barn wearing her red silk robe and her boots. She had a condom tucked in her pocket and a blanket in her arms. If he told her to leave, she'd give him the blanket so he could be more comfortable in his self-imposed exile.

The crescent moon didn't give her much light, but the barn doors were open and the glow from the floor lights saved her from tripping. She'd hate to fall and rip her bathrobe, which had set her back a tidy sum when she'd bought it at a trendy lingerie shop in Jackson.

The robe should have signaled to her that she was ready for a change of attitude. She'd bought it a few months ago when she couldn't stand her old, ratty terrycloth robe for another second. She'd meant to get a snuggly fake fur to keep her warm on cold winter nights, and instead she'd walked out of the store with this. It made her think of forbidden fantasies, and here she was, walking toward a barn that contained a man who knew all about those.

The closer she got to the open door, the faster her heart raced. She had never propositioned a man. She wasn't even sure if she could carry it off, but she'd walked all the way down here in semidarkness without tripping. Maybe a little adventure suited her, after all.

She ran through some potential greetings. *What's a cowboy like you doing in a barn like this? I'm researching the effects of a roll in the hay. Wanna help? Thought I'd save a horse and ride a cowboy tonight.* The last one was far too specific. She was becoming braver, but not that brave.

As she approached the door, she saw Drake walking down the barn aisle toward her. His face was in shadow. "I thought I heard someone out there."

"Just me." Faced with the actual Drake Brewster coming toward her, she forgot all the suggestive things she'd meant to say. Instead she totally wimped out. "I brought you a blanket." Worse yet, she held it in front of her like a shield. "How's Dottie?"

"No change." He stopped about five feet away from her. "Interesting outfit."

"Yes, well…I was in bed, and I heard you go outside again, so I figured you'd decided to sleep in the barn. And you might need a blanket." Wow, was she a temptress or what? Seduction City.

"Thoughtful of you."

"*Are* you planning to sleep in the barn?"

"Not really. I just decided to do one last check before going to bed. But I appreciate the effort."

"Oh." Shitfire! She could have stayed in his bed and everything would have gone as planned. Instead she was out here wearing boots and a bathrobe with a condom in her pocket. If they walked back to the house together, which now seemed likely, he'd go into his room and discover someone had been sleeping in his bed, and it sure as hell hadn't been Goldilocks.

"Did you *want* me to sleep in the barn?"

"Of course not, especially if there's no change with Dottie. That would be silly."

His gaze traveled over her. "Tracy, what's going on? Why are you out here wearing a red silk bathrobe?"

"How do you know it's silk?" As if that mattered, but she was surprised he'd guessed correctly.

"Silk has a distinctive way of draping a woman's body, especially when she's naked under it."

"You don't know that I'm naked!"

"Yes, I do."

Her cheeks grew hot. "Okay, so I'm naked. So I have a condom in my pocket and I came down here to seduce you. So what?"

"Oh, my God." He started to laugh but clapped a hand over his mouth immediately. Then he scrubbed that same hand over his face and cleared his throat. "Sorry, sorry. I'm not laughing at you, I promise."

"You are so laughing at me! You think I'm ridiculous. Which I am." She couldn't decide whether to run or stand her ground.

"You most certainly are not ridiculous. You're adorable. And sexy. And...could I please have that blanket?"

"Why?" She eyed him suspiciously.

"Because it's blocking my view."

That sounded promising, although she certainly couldn't claim to have engineered this seduction. If she had any talent for it, she'd have dropped the blanket a long time ago and slowly opened her robe.

He came closer and held out his hand. "Let me have it, please."

She released her death grip on the blanket. He took it from her and hung it over the nearest stall door. Meanwhile she could have started her vamp routine, but no, she just stood there waiting for him to make the next move.

He turned back to her. "That's much better. Now you can proceed."

"To do what?"

"Seduce me."

She gulped.

"It won't be tough to do. Imagining you naked under that silk, especially while you're wearing boots, is almost enough by itself."

"You're still laughing at me."

"Oh, no, I'm not, sweetheart. I'm putty in your hands. Whether you realize it or not, you have all the power. Own it."

7

DRAKE THOUGHT BRIEFLY of the assurances he'd given Josie Chance. But circumstances had changed. Tracy was outgrowing her fears, and he was the lucky bastard who got to be here now that she'd decided to spread her wings.

Or, more accurately, spread the lapels of her red silk robe. Fingers trembling, she untied the sash. Then slowly, ever so slowly, she opened the curtains on a show he would never forget if he lived to be a hundred.

His breath caught as the supple material slid away to reveal her creamy skin, inch by delicious inch. He glimpsed the inner swell of each breast, the valley between her ribs, the tempting indentation of her navel and the V of dark curls between her smooth thighs.

He dared not blink and miss a single moment. She was doing this for him, the man she'd been afraid to trust. And now she was ready to give him…everything. She parted the robe a little more, and her nipples emerged, rosy and tight.

They quivered as she drew in a shaky breath. "Say something."

He wasn't sure his vocal cords would work. "I'm… speechless." Sure enough, he sounded like a horny bullfrog. Felt like one, too. His cock pressed painfully against the ridge of his fly.

"Short but sweet." She swallowed. "I'll take it."

"Mmm." He'd always been proud of his gift of gab, for having a clever remark in any situation. Not this time. She was beautiful, but he'd been with beautiful women before. Although she'd dazzled him with her body, she'd blown him away with her bravery.

He couldn't imagine the raw courage she'd summoned to come down here wearing nothing but a silk robe and boots. Seeing any woman like that would have turned him on. Being confronted with Tracy in that getup was so unexpected that he clenched his fists against the urge to take her *now*.

But this was her show. That was the whole point, to let her test the limits of her sexuality. He wouldn't rob her of that. So he stood there as his slight tremors betrayed the strain of holding back.

Her gaze traveled over him and lingered on his crotch. When she lifted her head and looked into his eyes, her sultry smile was triumphant. "Parts of you are shouting."

"Yes, ma'am." He desperately wished she'd drop the robe and come closer, but if she wanted to draw out the torture, then somehow he'd keep from going crazy.

She reached into her pocket for the condom and held it out. "Mind this for me, okay?"

"How long?" It wasn't an idle question.

Her voice was as silky as her robe. "We'll see."

He might've groaned then. His brain was feeling fuzzy, and he couldn't be sure what he was doing anymore. He ached as he'd never ached, wondering if she had any idea what it cost him to take the foil packet from her outstretched hand without grabbing her and yanking her into his arms. As she tested her limits, she was sure as hell testing his. He'd never wanted a woman this much without acting on it.

"This is way more fun than I thought it would be." She allowed the robe to slither over her shoulders and drop to the floor of the barn. Then she braced her booted feet slightly apart, placed her hands on her rounded hips and sent him a challenging glance.

"Oh, yeah." He drank in the sight of her looking so strong, so proud. Her skin flushed and her nipples tightened as his gaze moved slowly from the fire in her eyes to her quivering breasts, down to her narrow waist and the womanly flare of her hips. When his attention traveled lower to the juncture of her thighs, heat shot through him at the glisten of moisture there. He wasn't the only one burning with anticipation.

She lifted one hand and crooked her finger. "Slowly."

He nodded, although *slow* didn't describe the way blood pounded through his veins or excitement zinged along every nerve in his body.

"Arms at your sides."

When he opened his mouth to protest, she shook her head. "I'm owning it, Drake."

So she was. He approached with his arms hanging at his sides as she'd instructed.

She held up one hand, palm facing him, like a traffic cop. "Close enough. I'll take it from here. Just… stand there."

He hoped he'd be able to obey that command as she stepped closer, her spicy perfume blending with the scent of aroused woman. At last she touched him, flattening her hands against his shirt, standing on tiptoe, and pressing her plump lips to his. Her mouth was open, her breath sweet and warm, her tongue… Oh, God, her tongue began to tease him, and his arms automatically went around her. It was pure reflex.

She pushed away from him, stepping out of his arms. "No." She sounded breathless. "Just kiss me. That's all."

Judging from her rapid breathing, he thought she might be losing a little of her iron control, but he nodded again and let his arms go limp. One part of him was the complete opposite of limp, though, and if she didn't do something about that soon, he couldn't be responsible for the consequences. She might hold all the cards, but he held the condom.

When she started kissing him again, he gripped the condom so tight the foil edge bit into his fingers. He was only vaguely aware of that, because he was too busy exploring the wonders of her mouth with his tongue, the only part of him she allowed free rein. She sighed and tilted her head, allowing him greater access. Then she moaned a little, and he knew they were making progress toward the goal.

Gently she unfastened his shirt. She made maddeningly slow progress. By the time she pulled it out of his waistband and massaged his bare chest, he was slippery with sweat. She moaned again and dug her fingertips into his pecs. If she didn't undo his jeans soon, he'd have to do it. A man could take only so much.

She was breathing hard, too, and glory be, she unhooked his belt and went to work on his jeans. Fortunately she didn't linger. When she slipped both hands under the waistband of his briefs and cupped him, he had to stop kissing her for fear he'd bite her tongue. It was that intense.

"Tracy, I need you." He could barely get the words out as he gulped for air. Her hands were stroking, massaging, creating pure havoc.

She wasn't in much better shape. "Okay." Panting, she shoved his briefs down and stepped back. "Put it on. Oh, Lordy, you are something to look at, Drake Brewster."

He'd been told that he was well endowed before, but he'd never been happier for the praise than now. He needed to please this woman as he'd never needed to please anyone before. She would remember tonight for the rest of her life, and he wanted her to remember that it was oh, so good.

He rolled on the condom. "What's the plan?"

"I didn't...get that far in my thinking."

If he'd had the breath to spare, he would have laughed. She'd managed this seduction all the way up to the critical part, but now she was out of ideas. He wasn't, though. He grabbed the blanket where he'd hung it on the stall door and tossed it on a nearby hay bale. "Sit there."

She did. Still wearing his jeans, sort of, he dropped to his knees in front of her. "Scoot forward. Good. Can I touch you now?"

"Oh, yes. Yes, *please.*"

"Excellent." He filled both hands with her smooth, hot bottom. "Lean back and brace yourself on your arms."

The motion lifted her breasts, and he was so tempted to nuzzle, to taste. But he had other things to do, very important things that involved making her come. Looking into her eyes, he nudged her thighs a little wider with his hips. "You surely did seduce me, lady."

Her eyes glowed with excitement. "I did, didn't I?"

"Yes, sweetheart, and this is what happens when you successfully seduce a man." Tightening his grip on her fanny, he probed her heat with his cock. She was so slick, he groaned. "Ready?"

She swallowed. "Yes."

Holding her gaze, he plunged into paradise. And held very still so he wouldn't come. Wow. Perfect.

Her eyes widened.

Instantly remorse hit him. Maybe he should have gone slower. "Did I hurt—"

"No! That was… Oh, Drake, you feel amazing."

He couldn't help but smile at that frank compliment. "Thank you, ma'am." How refreshing to know that Tracy would always tell him the truth, good or bad. This time, the truth was very, very good for his battered ego. "But we're just gettin' started."

"Speak for yourself." She tightened around his happy johnson. "I'm well on my way."

He sucked in a breath. "Easy."

"I've had easy." She squeezed him again. "Go for it, cowboy. And don't spare the horses."

If a man existed who could resist a challenge like that, Drake hadn't met him. He watched the light in her eyes grow brighter as he began to move, steadily increasing the pace until he was thrusting deep and fast. She held his gaze as if daring him to slow, daring him to come.

He would not. Not yet. Not until—there. A flash of sharp pleasure arced in those dark depths, a whimper escaped her parted lips, a tremor massaged his cock as he shot home again, and again. She was close.

His breathing was ragged, but he managed a warning. "I want you to come for me. But don't be loud about it, sweetheart."

She shook her head once, arched upward and came apart with a low, deep moan that was the sexiest thing he'd ever heard. The sound alone was enough to send him hurtling toward his own climax. He pushed in tight and let go, pulsing in rhythm with her, locked into her body, loving being there.

They stayed like that for several long seconds, neither of them moving, neither of them speaking. But he never stopped looking into her eyes. She made no attempt to hide…anything.

She seemed as caught up in the moment, as stunned by the intensity of it, as he was. Apparently she was brave enough to own the wonder of this moment just as she'd owned her power while seducing him. He'd never been with a woman this honest.

Sure, it scared him. He didn't know if he could handle that level of sharing, but he wanted to give it a try. His superficial way of relating to women was a bad habit that belonged to his past, not his future. She'd demonstrated that she could rid herself of old patterns. He would follow her lead.

When he finally spoke, gratitude tumbled out. "Thank you for walking down to the barn tonight. I expected to go to bed without resolving anything. I thought we'd tackle it in the morning."

She smiled. "We would have tackled it tonight, regardless."

"Oh?"

"If you hadn't headed down here for one last check on Dottie, you would have found me waiting in your bed."

That floored him. "You were in my room? When?"

"The whole time you ate dinner and cleaned up the kitchen. I thought you'd come to bed after that, and I'd…apologize in person."

"I'll be damned." He thought about that some more. "You were in my bed?"

"Yep."

"What were you wearing?" He wanted to complete the mental picture.

"Nothing."

He stared at her. "So we could have been doin' this in a cozy bed instead of in a barn full of horses?"

"Guess so."

"Damnation, woman. You should've given me a shout out or somethin'." But he couldn't help chuckling at the absurdity of it. "This has been memorable and all, but my knees are killing me."

"Then get up, for heaven's sake."

"I like being inside you." He couldn't remember ever admitting that to someone he'd just had sex with. It sounded needy, and he'd never wanted to appear that way.

But he'd said it now because Tracy inspired that kind of truth. Even better, he trusted her not to take advantage of his vulnerability. That was huge.

"That's nice to know, but you'll have to leave sometime. My arms can't hold me up much longer."

"Well, that shines a different light on things. I want you to be comfortable. Obviously we need to get going." He eased away from her. "Stay right there. I'll grab your robe."

Turning away, he used a handkerchief in his hip pocket to dispose of the condom, zipped up his pants and buckled his belt. Out here the cowhands carried bandanas, and if he ended up becoming a Westerner, he'd do the same. Was that his destiny?

He wished he knew, but at the present moment, his destiny wasn't a nagging problem. He was feeling contented, and that was an emotion he hadn't experienced in a while. He planned to enjoy it.

Tracy's robe was right where she'd dropped it, a splash of vivid color on the battered wooden floor. He picked it up and shook it out to get rid of any dust and bits of straw. A robe like this didn't belong on the floor of a barn, but he was mighty glad she'd worn it. He would never forget the picture she'd made coming in through the barn doors clutching that blanket to her chest.

He must have stood there for a minute reminiscing, because suddenly she was at his elbow. "I'll take it."

"I thought you were going to stay right—"

"No." She glanced up at him, her dark eyes sparkling. "You *told* me to stay right there. But I'm in the process of owning my power, so I didn't choose to listen."

He laughed. "Dear God, what sort of monster have I created?"

"The kind who will be lots more fun in bed."

That's when it occurred to him that what had happened between them could happen again. Multiple times, in fact. He'd moved into the guest room in order to keep an eye on a pregnant mare. But that didn't preclude keeping an eye on Tracy, who was fast becoming his favorite subject.

"So that condom you brought down here," he said casually. "Was that a single one you happened to come across, or…"

"There's an entire box sitting on your bedside table."

"Say no more, sweet lady. Let me check on Dottie one last time before we head on up to the house to count condoms."

"We'll still need to set an alarm."

"Absolutely. Dottie needs supervision. But I don't expect her to need constant supervision. You, on the other hand, very well might."

Tracy laughed, and the sound was light and carefree,

the laugh of a woman who'd had good sex and was expecting to have more of it.

Drake wasn't above taking some credit for that. He'd wondered if such intense physical stimulation would sabotage his determination to give Tracy the kind of experience she deserved. But her happiness had been so important that he'd managed to control his urges. She was definitely the kind of woman who was capable of making him a better man.

But he vowed not to think too far ahead. He'd been lucky enough to be in the right place at the right time to spend hours, maybe even days, with Tracy. He wouldn't get greedy, and he wouldn't start creating unrealistic expectations. They were together now, and that was great.

He fastened his shirt snaps as he walked down the aisle toward Dottie's stall. Probably a waste of time. Pretty soon he hoped to be completely naked and rolling around in his bed with Tracy. How funny that she'd lain in wait for him and he'd messed up her plan with his detour to the barn.

Smiling at the image of Tracy lying in his bed while he puttered around in the kitchen, he glanced into Dottie's stall. Then he went very still. She lay on her side in a bed of straw, her flanks heaving. He'd seen this often enough to know what was happening. Dottie was going into labor.

8

WHILE DRAKE ASSEMBLED the necessary supplies from Regan's truck, Tracy hurried back to the house to throw on some clothes and grab her smartphone to take pictures. She didn't want to meet this foal wearing nothing but a red silk robe and boots, and any new baby deserved photos.

Much as she'd looked forward to continuing her sexual adventure with Drake in the privacy of his bedroom, the thrill of an impending new life was damned exciting. Nerve-racking, too. If she'd had a working number for Jerry Rankin, she would have called him now. She was sad that he wouldn't be here.

At least Drake would be, and she had great confidence in him. He was far steadier and competent than she'd given him credit for when they'd first met, but she hadn't understood him then the way she did now. She wanted to learn more, because she suspected he'd acted out of character when he'd had sex with Regan's fiancée. That behavior didn't fit the man she knew.

Pulling on a worn pair of jeans and a T-shirt, she shoved her feet into her boots again. If those boots could talk… She shook her head and smiled. Drake would never let her forget how she showed up in the barn dressed the way she had been. For a brief moment she imagined talking about it years from now.

But that would mean they'd keep in touch. It would mean they'd maintain a relationship where talking about a wild night in the barn would make them laugh instead of cringe in embarrassment. It would mean neither of them would be with other people. It would mean… No, she wouldn't continue that line of thought. What a pointless thing to do at this stage.

She used the flashlight app on her phone to light her way to the barn. She could have done that earlier, but she hadn't wanted to announce her presence prematurely. She'd wanted to surprise him, and by God, she'd done that. In *so* many ways.

She chuckled, feeling a touch of pride as she relived those moments. She'd done it. She'd conquered her fears, at least for tonight, and experienced something remarkable. Lesson learned.

Once inside the barn, she switched off her flashlight app and quickly made her way down to the end stall. It was unlatched. Dottie still lay on her side breathing hard while Drake crouched near her head, stroking her and talking to her.

Tracy couldn't hear the words, but the low rumble of his voice sent warm shivers down her spine. "How's it going?" She hesitated to step into the stall. The process scared her more than a little, even though she wouldn't have missed it for anything.

Drake glanced up, his expression filled with a kindness and empathy that tugged at her heart. "She's coming along. Every time I see this, I thank God I'm not a woman. It's rough duty, giving birth."

"I thank God you're not a woman, too."

He grinned. "I appreciate that. How're you doin'?"

"Couldn't be better." She could elaborate on that and say she couldn't remember the last time she'd felt so alive, but she didn't want to gush, as if she'd never experienced sex that good. Which she hadn't.

His grin widened. "I'd go along with that, sweetheart. In fact, I—" He stopped talking as Dottie stirred and lumbered to her feet. "Guess she needs to move a bit."

"Is that normal?"

"Absolutely." He snapped a lead rope on her halter. "If you'll move back, I'll bring her out and walk her up and down the aisle."

"But what if she has her baby out here on the bare floor?"

"She won't." He started toward the front of the barn. "She'll let me know when she's ready to lie down again."

"Okay." It made Tracy nervous to see Dottie parading around when she needed to be settled on a bed of clean straw near the equipment Drake had laid out.

He turned and led the mare back toward Tracy. "You look worried. That foal isn't going to suddenly drop out of her with no warning, like a gum ball popping out of a machine."

That made her laugh. "I suppose not."

"Ever been in a maternity ward in the hospital?"

"Not as much as you might think. There's a growing tradition around here of having babies at home. But yes, I've been in one a time or two."

"Do you remember seeing pregnant women walking up and down the corridor?"

"I guess I have, now that you mention it."

"Same idea with a horse. Sometimes just lying there isn't the best plan. When a mare's in labor, it can feel better for her if she's able to move around. Isn't that right, Dottie?"

The mare snorted.

"I'll take that as a yes. Need another lap?"

Dottie paused by the stall door.

"Up to you." Drake smiled and stroked the mare's neck.

"You're enjoying this, aren't you?"

He glanced over at Tracy and blinked. "What makes you say that?"

"You're smiling, and you seem very relaxed and happy."

"That's partly your doing, sweetheart. And I could say the same about you."

She blushed. "Point taken."

"But you're right. I am enjoying myself, now that you mention it. Which is interesting, because lately I've been asking myself if I should continue being a vet."

"Why wouldn't you want to be a vet? You're obviously good at it."

"I'm a decent vet." He continued to stroke and scratch

Dottie's neck. "Not as gifted as my buddy Regan, but decent."

What an interesting admission. She wondered if she could coax him to say more. "You must be excellent or he wouldn't have left you in charge while he's gone."

"I'm fine for backup. But Regan's understanding of horses is exceptional. I admit I envy that ability." He glanced at her. "I can see the wheels turning."

"So you'll give up rather than compete with him?"

"No, nothing like that. Or I hope that wouldn't be my reason. And if you're dying to ask if my jealousy had something to do with what happened last Christmas…"

"It crossed my mind."

"The answer is yes, probably, to some extent. But it's not that simple."

Tracy didn't think so, either. She was about to ask another question when Dottie snorted even louder than before and stepped back into the stall.

"I think it might be showtime." Drake led her over to the bed of straw and unsnapped the lead rope. Dottie carefully dropped to her knees and rolled to her side. Then she rolled back and forth, groaning.

"Is she okay?"

"I'm sure it hurts, but this is normal." Drake unsnapped his cuffs and folded back his sleeves before putting on clear plastic gloves. "Poor girl. Bet you'll be glad when this is over." He stood back and gave Dottie plenty of room as she continued to grunt and roll.

Tracy hovered by the stall entrance. "Anything I can do?"

"My usual plan is to let nature take its course. If nature flakes out on me, then I'll move in and help things along. But for now, we let Dottie do her thing."

The mare finally stopped rolling and lay in the straw, her flanks heaving. Drake crouched down by her rump. He drew her tail aside and scooped away several handfuls of straw. "Here we go! Come on in here, Tracy. Get a better view."

She crept closer, heart pounding. Drake had done this countless times, so he probably wasn't the least bit worried. But she was the one who'd agreed to take this pregnant mare, and she desperately wanted everything to go well. She was torn between fascination with the process and the urge to bury her head in her arms until it was all over.

"See? Here come the forelegs." Drake's voice vibrated with excitement.

"Feet first?"

"If we're lucky, and it looks as if we are."

Sure enough, two sticks that apparently were legs emerged covered in what looked like a greased, semi-transparent garbage bag. Tracy held her breath.

"There's the nose. See it?"

Tracy leaned closer as a blunt, somewhat head-shaped form followed the spindly legs. "Yeah," she murmured. "Come on, Dottie. You're doing great."

"She is. She's pushing for all she's worth, and… there…the body, the hind legs, and…we're done!"

"What about that slimy thing?"

"We'll see if Dottie wants to handle that part, too. The less interference from me, the better. Let's give her a little more room." Drake edged away a few feet and Tracy followed his example.

Dottie lay still for a moment, still breathing hard. Then she lifted her head and gazed down the length of her body.

"Your foal is right there, girl," Drake crooned. "You did a mighty fine job. Want to finish up?"

As if she'd understood every word, Dottie maneuvered until she could lick the foal.

"Incredible." Tracy watched as the little creature gradually was freed of its covering. "It looks like her!"

"It does, indeed." Drake moved closer. "Will you let me take care of the cord, sweetie? That's a good girl." He handled the job with brisk efficiency and then checked between the foal's legs. "Colt."

"A son. Dottie has a son." Tracy couldn't help thinking of how proud Jerry Rankin would be. She'd make it her job to track him down. He should at least have visiting privileges.

Drake gathered up his instruments. "Glad I didn't have to use most of these. When everything goes according to plan, I don't. This birth was pure pleasure."

"I'm glad, for many reasons." Tracy straightened. "And I don't know what I would have done without you here. The minute she started rolling around, I'd have been beside myself."

He shrugged. "You would have called the guy from Jackson."

"And he would have taken a good hour to get here. By then it would have been all over. Even if it had gone well, I wouldn't have known whether it was going well or not. I would have been a basket case." She gazed at him. "Minimize your contribution if you must, but I won't."

He gave her a lopsided smile. "You sound serious about that."

"I am." She didn't return his smile. "You rode in here like a knight in shining armor and saved the day. I'm incredibly grateful that you did, and I'm prepared to let people around here know that they've judged you unfairly."

"Whoa, whoa! You're going to start a campaign to get the residents of this town to *like* me? That would be embarrassing as hell. Don't you dare."

"I'll be subtle about it."

"I don't know how subtle you can be once they figure out we spent the night together."

She frowned. "You make that sound as if you're leaving after tonight."

"For your sake, I probably should. Maybe we can convince everyone I was only here for the birth of the foal and we were too busy taking care of that to get horizontal."

"I don't care if they know we got horizontal, although technically, that hasn't happened yet. I'm still hoping."

He chuckled and glanced up at the rafters. "Oh, Tracy. You do have a way about you."

"You, too. And a killer accent."

His green eyes danced as he met her gaze. "And you accuse *me* of being charming. If you keep making remarks like that, you'll make it impossible for me to resist you."

"Booya!"

"Tracy…" He laughed and shook his head.

"And I do want to set people straight about you. I wish they could have seen you tonight with Dottie. These are horse people, Drake. They'd respect the way you dealt with her, how patient you've been the whole time. It would go a long way toward repairing the damage. Please don't tell me I can't mention what you've done here tonight."

His eyebrows lifted. "*All* of what I've done?"

"No, of course not. The vet part. Not the action on the hay bale. That's our business."

"Good luck with that. Apparently you've forgotten that I have a reputation around these parts, and everyone will assume I won you over with lots of good sex, and that's the only reason you've become my biggest fan all of a sudden."

"But *I* seduced *you*."

"Are you going to tell them that?"

She had to admit that didn't sound like a good idea. "I'd like to keep sex out of the discussion. This is about you getting a fair shake in this town because you're not the villain everyone thinks you are."

"They know Regan has forgiven me, right?"

"Well, yeah."

He spread his arms. "There you go. They know the wronged party has moved past the incident, but that doesn't matter. They think Regan is going too easy on me." He paused. "You thought so."

"I know, but that was before—"

"Tracy, it's a wonderful impulse, but I don't think

having you sing my praises is going to help, especially because you're the town sweetheart and they'll assume I've despoiled you."

"Despoiled? Who uses that word anymore?"

"Me. It's one of my closely guarded secrets. I actually liked my English classes. I dug Shakespeare and even thought the sonnets were cool. I, um, have been known to write my own poetry. Which no one has ever seen, by the way." He peered at her as if he'd just confessed to occasionally committing murder.

She was stunned, both by the fact he was a closet romantic and that he'd never revealed it before. "No one?"

"Nope."

"Where do you keep it?"

"I have some journals in the cabin."

"Would you...let me read them?"

He gazed at her for a long time. "I don't know. Maybe. Let me think about it."

"Okay." At least he hadn't flatly refused.

He broke eye contact and turned his attention to Dottie and her foal. "You know, if we're not careful, we'll miss the magic when the little guy first gets to his feet."

She took her cue. He was through delving into his most personal issues for now. "Can't have that! I specifically brought my phone to record it."

"Then get ready, because his momma's looking to get up, and once she does, she'll coax her son to do the same."

Tracy focused her lens on the foal. "He seems so fragile. Can he really stand on those legs?"

"He has to if he wants to eat, and believe you me,

he wants to eat. That'll be his primary goal for quite a while. It's the way everything's set up. Foals have to stand to eat, which in the wild means they'll soon be ready to run if a predator comes along."

"I'm glad that won't be a problem for Sprinkles."

"Sprinkles? Is that his name?"

"I think it is." She held the phone steady and snapped a couple of shots of the foal lying in the straw. "He looks like vanilla ice cream with sprinkles."

"So he does." Drake sounded amused.

"But you have a vote. If you have a name to propose, go right ahead. Without you, he might not even be here."

"I like Sprinkles. Do you think we need to give Regan and Lily a vote?"

"Maybe, but let's not. Let's just announce that his name is Sprinkles. We were here at the critical moment, so I think that gives us naming privileges." As she gazed at her phone's screen, Dottie's nose appeared. She nudged the foal. "Is this it?"

"This is it." Drake came to stand next to her. "You'll text these to me, right?"

"You bet." She took shot after shot as Dottie coaxed her wobbly foal to test those toothpick legs against the pull of gravity.

She didn't realize she was cheering softly until Drake joined in. They stood there like a couple of proud parents urging a toddler to walk. When he was finally standing on those impossibly long legs, they both uttered a muted cheer, one guaranteed not to startle the little guy and cause him to lose his balance.

Tracy got a few more shots of Sprinkles nursing before she turned off her camera. "So sweet. Should we give them some privacy?"

"Not quite yet. I have to stick around and make sure Dottie passes the placenta, but if you're tired, go on back up to the house."

She shook her head. "If you're staying, I'm staying."

"It won't be very interesting from here on out. The drama is over."

"I'll get to be with you, right?"

"Yes, but I won't be a lot of fun. I need to monitor these two and make sure everything's fine, so if you brought another condom down, I wouldn't be able to—"

"Are you suggesting that all I can think about when I'm with you is sex?"

He gave her a lazy grin. "Just for the record, I wouldn't blame you for that. It's quite a compliment, when you stop to think about it."

"Well, just for the record, I would love to stay down here and talk with you, even if we can't have sex."

He met her gaze. "That's an even bigger compliment. Thank you, Tracy."

"You're welcome. I'll go get the blanket and make us a nice place to sit. And then we can discuss why you're considering giving up your profession."

He groaned at that, but she ignored him. Drake Brewster needed to exorcise his demons, and she was just the person to help him do it.

9

DRAKE HAD GROANED partly because he thought Tracy expected him to. Secretly he was relieved to have someone willing to discuss what he should do with his life. The men in his family weren't supposed to have doubts, and if they did, they knocked back a few shots of bourbon and forgot about their worries. As the only son of a man who'd always been cloaked in absolute certainty, Drake had never felt free to be unsure.

While he examined mother and foal for any signs of stress, Tracy arranged their seating. He came out to discover she'd doubled the blanket and laid it alongside the outer wall of the stall. She sat on one side of it, her arms wrapped around her bent knees.

She freed one hand to pat the spot next to her. "Take a load off, cowboy."

"I love having you call me that." He dropped down beside her and sat cross-legged. "But much as I like it, I don't qualify."

"Sure you do." She glanced over at him. "You know

your way around horses and you look good in the clothes. You'll pass."

The woman sure could make him laugh. "But I can't twirl a rope and I've never ridden in a Western saddle. Just English."

"We can fix that tomorrow." She picked up her phone and looked at the time. "Or more accurately, today. But you are missing one critical component of cowboyness."

"I'm probably missing several, but what one are you thinking about?" Feet in front of him, he relaxed against the wooden wall behind them. Tonight he'd made love to a woman and watched over the delivery of a healthy foal. Good stuff.

"You don't have a hat. Or if you do, I've never seen it on you."

He turned his head to look at her. She looked right back, her dark eyes warm, her expression open and accepting. That made him feel like a million bucks. "You're right. I don't own a cowboy hat."

"Why not?"

He couldn't help smiling. She was so damned cute. She'd put her hair back in its ponytail, probably so it wouldn't be in her way during the foaling. "I thought we were going to discuss my next career move."

"We can in a minute, but I'm curious about the hat thing. I've watched plenty of folks come out to this part of the world, and if they like it here, they usually pick up a hat, even if they're not planning to stay. You haven't bought one."

"I guess it's a fair question." He savored the feeling of being able to talk to her without worrying what she'd think. "I believe a hat signifies something important, and as I said, I don't qualify."

She took some time to absorb that. "Regan would probably teach you to rope, and two of these horses need to be ridden, so you could check that box fairly easily, too."

"I hadn't thought of asking Regan to teach me roping. Might be fun."

"Then you could get a hat."

Resting his head against the wall and closing his eyes, he thought about it, but even if he learned to throw a rope and spent some time in a Western saddle, he still couldn't picture himself wearing the hat. "Don't think so. A baseball cap is all I need."

"A cowboy hat is more practical. It shades your eyes and the back of your head. Plus it looks really cool."

"I know, but..." He tried to identify where his resistance came from, because she was right about the practical side of a Western hat. When it suddenly hit him, he sucked in a breath. Yeah, that was it.

"What?"

"When I was a kid, I liked cowboy movies. I even watched the old ones on cable, the ones where you could tell the good guys because they wore the white hats."

She didn't say anything, but her hand found his. She interlaced their fingers and held on.

"I admired everything about those guys. They were champions of the weak, they were honest to a fault, and...loyal to their friends." It physically hurt his throat to say that last part, but he forced himself.

She squeezed his hand.

"I don't deserve to wear that hat, Tracy." When he felt her move and let go of his hand, he opened his eyes.

She quickly straddled his knees and took his face in both hands. "Yes, you do." And she kissed him.

It was the sweetest, most loving gesture any woman had ever made to him. It spoke of caring and empathy, of encouragement and respect. He wrapped both arms around her and simply held her as he received her blessing—he couldn't think of a better word for it—in the spirit it was intended. This wasn't about heat and hunger. It was about redemption.

Slowly she ended the kiss and settled back on his knees. He opened his eyes to find her watching him, her smile soft. "What do you say now, cowboy?"

"Okay." His voice was still hoarse with emotion. "I'll consider getting a hat."

She shook her head. "Not good enough. *Considering* means you're still in the thinking stage."

"What is this, a project?"

"I think it is, yes. You would look great in a hat, and I know exactly what we're going to do."

"Oh?" He liked the way she'd said *we,* as if they shared this project. "And what are *we* going to do, Miss Tracy?"

"We're going shopping."

"Oh, no, we're not. If you help me pick out a hat in the Shoshone General Store, the gossip will fly. It may anyway, but that would ramp it up considerably. I can hear it now. *Nice hat. Understand Tracy picked it out for you. How are things going between you guys?* Wink, wink, nudge, nudge."

"I wasn't thinking we'd buy it here. I have to work from eleven to five tomorrow. Then I need to feed the critters, but after that, assuming Dottie and Sprinkles are doing fine, we'll take a quick drive to Jackson. The stores are keeping summer hours. We can make it there before they close and be home again in a jiffy." She grinned. "With a hat."

She looked so proud of her idea that he couldn't imagine saying no. "All right. I'll drive us into Jackson."

"Yay!"

Here she'd given him a gift by proposing this trip, and yet she acted as if he'd given her one by agreeing to go. He knew himself. Left to his own devices, he'd never buy a hat, even if he thought he was worthy of one. "But only if Dottie and Sprinkles are doin' fine."

"They will be." She climbed off him. "Let's take a look and see how they're doing now."

"Good call. Maybe Dottie's delivered the placenta by now." He hoped so. He couldn't speak for Tracy, but he was tired. She had to be, too.

Tracy stood and peered over the chest-high enclosure. "Aw, Drake. They're sleeping."

He joined her, and it was the most natural thing in the world to put his arm around her as they gazed at the tender scene in the stall. Sprinkles had curled up in the shelter of his mother's body, and both mare and foal were asleep.

Watching them, he felt a sense of accomplishment, and with it came another epiphany. He really did love working with horses. Whether he continued as a vet or not, he needed horses in his life. He might not be the horse whisperer Regan was, but he treasured working with them, anyway.

"That's just precious," Tracy murmured.

Precious wasn't a word he generally used, but they were darned cute. Sharing the moment with Tracy was pretty special, too, almost as if they were proud parents peeking into the nursery. He hated to disturb the magic of holding her against his side while they contemplated the miracle of a newborn foal, but she would want a picture of this. He should probably remind her to take one. She seemed mesmerized by the scene, though. Then she slid her arm around his waist and laid her head on his shoulder.

His chest tightened with an emotion he wasn't all that familiar with. To hell with the picture. If she didn't mention it, he wouldn't either. He'd rather stay right like this.

In fact, he wouldn't move if someone offered him a million bucks. Tracy had told him without words that she didn't just lust after him anymore. She might still display that hair-trigger response under the right circumstances, but at the moment, she was communicating clearly that she *liked* him.

Earlier in the evening they'd become lovers, and that had been a big turning point in their relationship. But in the past few hours something more had passed between them, and they'd become friends. He valued the second stage even more than the first one, and he'd been crazy about that first one.

She snuggled closer. "I should get a picture."

"Guess so."

"But I hate to move."

"Me, too."

"This has been an awesome night, Drake. The kind of night that I'll remember for a long time."

"So will I." He kissed the top of her head. "Thank you."

She sighed happily. "I should thank *you,* but then we'd start that silly thing where we compete to see who gets in the last thank-you."

"How do you know we'd do that?" He rested his cheek on the top of her head. "Maybe you'd say, *No, I should thank you,* and I'd say, *You're right. You should.*"

"I doubt it. That's not you."

"Try me."

"Okay, I will. No, Drake, I should be thanking *you,* because you're so wonderful and generous and—"

"Yep, I surely am. I'm amazing. In fact, I'm so special I think I'll get me a hat."

She started laughing, which broke up their cozy little moment, but he was okay with that. They were both getting slaphappy from fatigue. With any luck, Dottie had passed the placenta and he and Tracy could go to bed. That was an enticing prospect. He didn't want to fall asleep and miss all the fun they could have.

Back in the stall, he located the placenta and tossed it into the bucket he'd brought for it. Dottie and Sprinkles continued to snooze as Tracy took a few more pictures.

Then she turned. "Are we ready to go?"

"Whenever you are." He peeled off his gloves and set the bucket outside the stall. He'd deal with that later. "They'll be fine for a few hours."

She covered a yawn and glanced at her phone. "We have another three hours before it's feeding time again."

"Then let's close up and head out." Moments later they'd latched both the back and front doors of the barn. He caught her hand in his as they walked up to the house in the slight chill. Stars winked overhead and the crescent moon had already set. "I'll set my alarm and feed," he said. "You have to be at work by eleven, but I can nap."

"That's not right. Feeding the critters is what Lily and Regan are paying me for."

"Yes, but circumstances have changed, so we have to be flexible. Besides, if you don't sleep in, you'll be too tired to go hat shopping."

"You drive a tough bargain, Brewster." She covered her mouth with her free hand as another yawn overtook her.

That second yawn convinced him that he should rethink his original plan for what would happen when they got back to the house. "Listen, maybe you should go back to your room so you can get some decent rest."

"What?" She pulled him to a halt. "Are you kicking me out of your room?"

"Of course not! But you're obviously tired, and if we both end up in my room, I may not be able to let you go straight to sleep, which you should, because you need your—"

"Shut up, cowboy."

"Excuse me?"

"Just be quiet until we get to your room, okay? And then the only things I want to hear out of you are gasps and moans of ecstasy. None of this *you need your rest* garbage. Understood?"

"Yes, ma'am." Suddenly he wasn't the least bit tired.

"I guess you can also say *yes, ma'am* now and then, because that Southern drawl turns me on like you wouldn't believe. No more being solicitous, though. I've been waiting to climb into bed with you for hours. Hay bales are fine once in a while, but I wouldn't want a steady diet of having sex on them."

Neither would he, but he didn't say so. He was saving his breath for all those gasps and moans of ecstasy she'd promised him. Apparently the switch Tracy had flipped to give herself a change of attitude had been permanently turned on. And he was loving it.

"I will, however, let you feed the critters so I can sleep in. You make an excellent point about the shopping trip, and I need to be sharp for that. There's an art to choosing the right hat, especially the first one. Eventually you'll get a feel for how to choose them on your own."

He grinned. "Yes, ma'am."

"That's what I like. A Southern gentleman in an agreeable mood. I can't wait to get you naked."

He was laughing, now, because he so enjoyed listening to her being sassy. But as they climbed the steps together and went into the house, he realized that he'd semicommitted to staying at least through tomorrow night. He doubted they'd come home from a hat-shopping trip and not want to celebrate the event appropriately, which would be in his bed.

But if Dottie and Sprinkles continued to do well, he

had no official reason to stay after that. The mare had foaled and Tracy was no longer afraid of her sexuality. If he stayed beyond tomorrow night, word would surely get out.

After that, he could reasonably predict that someone, most likely Josie, would demand to know his intentions. After all, he'd told her he wouldn't be getting involved with Tracy. Unfortunately, he had no idea what his intentions were.

At least he had no idea for the future. The present was crystal clear, especially after Tracy drew him into the guest bedroom and clothes began flying everywhere. He couldn't have talked, even if she hadn't forbid him to. He was too busy kissing whatever wonders he uncovered.

He was particularly focused on her plump breasts. He'd denied himself the pleasure of touching and licking them when he'd made love to her in the barn, but he planned to correct that omission now. Once they were both stripped down to nothing, he tumbled her back onto the bed, cupped that glorious bounty in both hands, and feasted.

Moaning, she arched into his caress, which sent desire shooting through his veins. He couldn't seem to get enough of her. After putting up with a blanket tossed onto a hay bale, having her stretched out on the bed, where he had access to every bit of her, made him determined not to miss a single inch of soft, moist skin.

She was delicious everywhere, but when he slid down between her thighs and tasted her essence, desire ripped through him with a tsunami-like force. She writhed beneath him as she responded to the lap of his tongue and the thrust of his fingers. She came, and then she came again, her cries filling the room.

He loved hearing those lusty sounds, loved knowing she could make all the noise she wanted this time. He lingered in that sweet valley as she trembled in the aftermath. Her scent intoxicated him, and although his cock was stiff as granite, although his balls ached for release, he leaned forward and swiped his tongue over her pulsing center. Maybe once more.

She gasped and clutched his head as she struggled for breath. "Come…here." She tugged.

He eased up her sweat-dampened body and hovered over her, his forearms taking most of his weight.

She looked up at him, her dark eyes glazed with pleasure. "That was…" She smiled. *"Good."*

"I'm glad." He leaned down and brushed his mouth over hers so she could share the taste. Then he watched as she licked her lips. He had to clench his jaw against the urge to come. Once he had himself under control, he cleared his throat. "Can I talk, now?"

"Uh-huh." She dragged in air. "But first, get the box."

He didn't have to ask what she meant. There was only one box that mattered, the one that had been sitting on the nightstand when they'd walked into the room. Fortunately he could reach it without much effort. He set it down between her breasts. "Here."

She pulled a packet out and handed it to him. "Here."

Grinning, he pushed himself to a sitting position straddling her thighs, ripped open the packet and handed her the unwrapped condom. "Here." This was fun. He picked up the box and leaned slightly forward so he could return it to the nightstand while putting his cock within her reach.

He'd thought he was being so clever, so cute. Then she fumbled the job. Not completely, because she got the thing on him, but in the process he had flashbacks to his teen years when he'd had the control of a gnat. Giggling hysterically might have been part of her problem. He didn't think it was so damn funny, and neither would she if this condom application went bad.

Finally she snapped it in place. "There."

He spoke through gritted teeth. "Thanks."

"Your face is all scrunched up."

"No kidding."

"Did I get it on right? Maybe I should adjust—"

"Don't touch."

"If you say so." Laughter rippled through her voice. "Are we going to do this, then?"

"In a minute."

"Okay."

Gradually the pounding in his groin let up enough that he unclenched his jaw and opened his eyes.

She stared up at him, all innocence except for the sparkle of mischief lurking in her eyes.

"Tracy, did you do that on purpose?"

Her smile confirmed his suspicions. "You started it," she said. "I just ended it."

"You almost *did* end it." He moved between her soft thighs, grateful that he'd held on, in spite of her. His reward would be worth everything she'd put him through.

"Just proving a point."

"What point?" He knew the territory well, now, and he found her slick heat without effort. After two orgasms, she was drenched. He held back, poised at her entrance, knowing that once he thrust deep, his brain would cease to function, and he wanted to hear this.

"A cowboy only fires when ready. More evidence that you qualify."

"Damnation, woman! You're makin' this up as you go along."

"Ask any cowboy. They'll say it's true."

"I guarantee they would, sweetheart. No man would admit to anything less, cowboy or stockbroker."

She ran her hands down his back and bracketed his hips. "Just want to make sure you're still getting that hat."

"I don't know. You'd better check out my other qualifications before we go shopping."

"Such as?"

He surged forward, burying himself in her hot channel as she gasped in surprise. Breathing hard, he gazed down at her. "Is that the cowboy way?"

She gulped. "Yes."

"How about this?" He began a slow, deliberate rhythm and watched the fire build in her eyes. "Is that how cowboys do it?"

"Uh-huh."

"Then what?" He shifted his angle and picked up the pace. "Like this?"

"Oh, *yeah*." She clutched his hips and held on as her

breasts jiggled with the impact of each thrust. "Just like that."

He scooped one arm under her bottom and lifted her just enough to let him go deeper. "Then maybe this."

She didn't answer him this time, but her body did. The first spasm rolled over his cock, then the second.

"Come for me, Tracy." He felt her give way. "That's it, darlin'. *Now.*"

She erupted in his arms, and he followed her right down that tumbling waterfall of sensation. His cries blended with hers as he surrendered to a climax that shook him to his soul. If this was the cowboy way, he was all for it.

10

TRACY FELL ASLEEP in Drake's arms, his body still locked securely with hers. Obviously that situation had changed at some point, because when her phone alarm went off, she was by herself in his bed. She stretched and foolishly wished he'd been there beside her when she'd opened her eyes.

That wouldn't have worked out too well, though. She was still naked, and thoughts of him brought a rush of arousal to all the places he'd loved so energetically hours earlier. If he'd been there, she would have been tempted to replay some of those excellent moments.

But she had to go to work. As she sat up, she noticed a note anchored by the box of condoms sitting on the nightstand. He'd scribbled it in haste and he wrote in cursive, not the neat block letters she'd noticed many men preferred. His handwriting was horrible, and she had to squint to figure out some of the words, but she managed it.

Dottie and Sprinkles doing great. Critters all fed.

Coffee in the carafe if you want it. Drove home for a few things. Back around noon. Will start feeding at five. See you after work. I just realized I don't know where you live. I mean normally.

He'd signed it *D*. No tender closing. The man had admitted to writing poetry, but there wasn't anything poetic about this note. If she'd hoped for something sweet, something to let her know...what? That he was madly in love with her? That would be a little quick, now, wouldn't it? She'd be suspicious of a love note this soon.

Or so she told herself. Still, the utilitarian message he'd left, and the very fact he hadn't waited until she woke up to drive away, didn't make her feel all warm and fuzzy. She wouldn't have minded if he'd signed his note *Warmly* or *Fondly*. He'd been both warm and fond in the barn and in this bed.

He'd been one hot commodity, too. Whew. If he'd been popular with women in the past, and she believed that he had, then experience counted for something. He'd given her more pleasure in a few hours than her other two serious boyfriends had given her...ever. They'd never come close to making her yell. In this room, in this bed, with Drake, she'd yelled. Loudly.

Maybe loud yelling didn't translate into flowery love notes. If she had to choose, she'd take sex that prompted shouts of joy over those notes. No contest there. Plus he had asked where she lived, which had a promising ring to it, as if he might want to continue seeing her after the house-sitting gig ended.

After all they'd shared, she found it odd that he didn't know that simple fact about her. She rented a small apartment above Spirits and Spurs from Josie. Josie had lived there originally, and after she'd moved to the Last Chance, Caro Davis had stepped in to help run the bar. Caro had also rented the apartment because it was so close to work.

Now married, Caro and former Chicago Cubs star Logan Carswell traveled the country, using Logan's invested earnings to do good works. Logan ran baseball clinics for disadvantaged kids and Caro supervised quilting circles in senior centers.

Tracy had grabbed the apartment the minute Caro had moved out. She loved living in the middle of the tiny town where she'd grown up. Before she started her shift, she'd check on her houseplants. She glanced at the digital clock on her phone. Time to get moving.

She'd rather not have to explain being late. She wasn't good at lying, and because of her caretaking chores at Peaceful Kingdom, she couldn't use oversleeping as a legitimate excuse. That would imply she'd neglected the animals.

After quickly making the bed, she returned to her own room to shower and dress. Lily and Regan's bed was a king and more suited for wild sex, but Tracy had made a decision to keep the action in the guest room. That seemed more respectful. Drake hadn't questioned her choice, and she'd bet that he'd agree with her. Southern manners and all that.

Having him gone felt strange, which wasn't the least bit logical. He hadn't arrived to check on Dottie until late in the afternoon, so he'd been on the premises less than twenty-four hours. It seemed longer, no doubt because of all they'd experienced. And all they'd talked about.

She hoped he wouldn't back out of the shopping trip. She'd never known a man who loved to buy clothes, and a hat was an article of clothing. For Drake, though, it was far more than that. She'd stumbled into that discussion out of pure curiosity, and thank goodness she had. He'd helped her leap the boundaries of her comfort zone, and maybe she could help him forgive himself enough to buy a hat.

Holding that thought, she hurried down to the barn to make sure Dottie and Sprinkles were doing fine. They were snuggled together, both sound asleep, so she hopped in her little white truck and drove to Spirits and Spurs. It wasn't a muscular truck, but it ran well and people in Shoshone tended to drive pickups. She felt more a part of the community having a truck instead of a sedan.

She adored this quaint town with its one stoplight and a typical main street lined with a few established businesses. Shoshone had a diner, a general store, a gas station, a real-estate office, an ice-cream parlor and the bar. Folks who needed to do serious shopping went to Jackson about an hour away, just as she and Drake planned to do tonight.

Congratulating herself on coming up with a plan that would give them some anonymity on their outing, she pulled into the side parking lot next to Spirits and Spurs. Josie's truck was there, so her employer must have decided to work on the books today. Maybe she'd brought Archie in. Tracy adored that little towhead. Archie was the only person in the world who could turn Jack Chance into mush. It was fun to watch.

She entered the bar through the front door, which all the employees did except Josie. The building was old and the design was quirky. The only back door opened straight into Josie's office. That meant at closing time all the garbage had to be taken through there, and all food supplies came in through her office, too.

Josie kept talking about remodeling, but that would require some structural changes that would permanently alter the look and feel of the bar. Nobody wanted that.

Some said that the "spirits" who'd inspired Josie to change the name of the bar would stage a revolt if she remodeled. It was said that the bar was haunted by the ghosts of miners and cowboys who'd patronized it during its century-long existence. Tracy had never seen a ghost, but she knew people who swore that they had, including Josie.

The bar wasn't busy at eleven in the morning, either with live guests or dearly departed ones. The lunch rush would start in another hour. Archie's cheerful little voice piped up from the office and Tracy smiled. She'd take a minute to say hello before starting her shift.

At age two and a half, Archie was speaking in complete sentences and getting into everything. Tracy admired Josie for bringing him to her office, where he could quickly create chaos if she turned her back on him for even a second. But Josie seemed to have a sixth sense about that.

Peeking through the office door, Tracy discovered her boss wasn't trying to work, after all. She sat at her desk with Archie on her lap while he colored enthusiastically on blank sheets of paper Josie had provided.

"Looks like Rembrandt in training," Tracy said.

Josie glanced up. "Maybe. I'm thinking he's more of an impressionist."

Archie finished drawing with a purple crayon and held up his picture. "I made a *doggie*."

Tracy gave him thumbs-up. "You totally did, Archie!"

The little boy turned the paper around and nodded with satisfaction at what he saw. "Yup. I totally did." He mimicked Tracy's thumbs-up before grabbing another piece of paper so he could start his next masterpiece.

Josie sent Tracy a look. "Does that attitude remind you of anybody?"

"Yep." Tracy smiled.

"It's as if Jack spit him right out of his mouth."

Archie looked up and giggled. "You're silly, Mommy!"

"I get it from you, you little munchkin." Josie blew a raspberry against his cheek.

He giggled some more. "Stop it, Mommy. I gotta work."

"Yeah, me, too," Tracy said. "See you guys later." She turned to leave.

"Just a sec, Tracy. I wanted to ask you about something."

With a sense of foreboding, Tracy faced her boss. "What's that?" But she knew.

"I understand you have a pregnant mare out at Peaceful Kingdom."

Tracy gulped. Then she stammered. All in all, she

reacted exactly like someone who had been doing something clandestine. And the whole story was about to come out.

"I took her in yesterday. How did you know?"

Something flickered in Josie's blue eyes. "A guy named Jerry Rankin came into the bar last night to ask around and find out if anyone knew of a job."

"He came here? Do you have a contact number for him?" Maybe this wasn't such a disaster, after all, if Josie had a number for Jerry.

"He's at the Last Chance. Jack put him on the payroll temporarily. He wasn't happy that the guy dumped a mare about to foal on an unsuspecting house sitter. Jerry admitted he knew the foal could come any minute, which was one of the main reasons he brought her to you."

"He knew that? I wish he'd told me."

"He was afraid if he did, you wouldn't take her. In his defense, he didn't fully understand the awkward situation he was sticking you with. He just knew he didn't have the resources to deal with it. Jack wanted me to ask you about the mare when you came in today."

"Well, she's fine." Tracy felt her cheeks warm. "She delivered her foal last night."

Josie swore, and then quickly covered Archie's ears, as if she could keep him from hearing. "Sorry, munchkin."

"It's okay, Mommy."

"So she foaled." The sharpness in Josie's blue eyes didn't match her casual pose. "But surely you didn't try to handle that yourself."

"No, but since I'd taken in an animal against Regan and Lily's instructions, I didn't want to call the vet in Jackson because that would cost a bunch of money."

"You called Drake Brewster."

"Yes." Tracy took a shaky breath. "He did a terrific job, Josie. He's a good guy who made a terrible mistake. I think maybe we should all—"

"I agree with you."

"You *do?* I thought everybody at the Last Chance hated Drake."

Archie held up another picture that looked pretty much like the previous one. "I made a kitty!"

Tracy summoned up a cheerful comment. "You did, Archie! That's a great kitty!"

Archie shrugged. "I know." He grabbed another sheet of paper.

Josie glanced down at her son. "You know what, buddy? I think you need to relocate to the bar. You can show Steve your pictures, okay? I'm sure he'd love to see your work."

"Okay." Archie seemed perfectly happy to attract a new audience.

Josie gathered his supplies and took him by the hand. "Don't go away," she said to Tracy as she herded the little boy out the door. "I'll be right back once I get him settled with Steve."

"My shift's about to start." Steve could handle the bartending duties for a while, but Tracy liked to organize her supplies before the rush began and she and Steve were both frantic to fill orders. Besides, she didn't look forward to the coming discussion.

"I know, but hardly anyone's out there. And this is important."

That was what Tracy was afraid of. She didn't want to have an *important* discussion about Drake.

Josie came back in, and instead of sitting behind her desk, she leaned against the front of it. "I won't kid you. Drake doesn't have a lot of fans out at the ranch. But I always think there are two sides to every story, so yesterday I paid him a visit. That's when I first found out about the pregnant mare. Jerry Rankin only confirmed what I already knew."

"You went to see Drake?" Drake had failed to mention that important incident. It wasn't quite lying, but it wasn't exactly being open, either. Her stomach churned.

"I'm guessing from your expression that he didn't tell you about that. Good for him. I specifically asked him not to, because I knew you wouldn't appreciate that I'd gone over there."

"Why would I mind? In fact, I'm glad you were willing to make friends with him." So Drake had been keeping his word to Josie by not saying anything. Tracy felt a little better, but she wondered why Josie had made him promise to keep quiet. She wasn't sure she wanted to know.

"I am willing to be his friend on the condition that he doesn't do something stupid regarding you. You were my main motivation for going over there."

Tracy groaned. "Josie…"

"Okay, I'm guilty of meddling. I admit it. But I could tell you were fascinated with him, and he doesn't have a good record when it comes to women."

"He made *one* mistake."

"Maybe that's true, but I've met the man. He's charming as hell. I understand the type, because Jack's a lot like him, and years ago, Jack had a terrible record when it came to women."

"But look how well that all turned out for you and Jack!"

Josie took a deep breath. "I said Drake reminds me of Jack, but he's different in two important ways. Jack had roots. No matter what, he wasn't going anywhere. After his dad died, Jack had focus, too, because he had to step up and keep the ranch on an even keel. By Drake's own admission, he doesn't have any direction, but he's not planning to go back to Virginia, so he has no roots, either."

"That doesn't mean he won't get those things." Tracy hated hearing what she knew was the truth. She'd even told herself that Drake could end up breaking her heart and that she was okay with taking the risk. But hearing it spoken aloud by Josie, a woman whose judgment she trusted, made her wonder how okay she would really be if Drake left her high and dry. And he might.

"Maybe he'll settle into a groove eventually," Josie said. "But he's not a very good bet right now when he's flailing around. I went over there basically to ask him to leave you alone. He said he'd already planned to do that."

"Josie!" Tracy's cheeks grew hot with a combination of humiliation and anger. Josie was her boss, so she had to be careful not to be disrespectful, but…how dare she do that!

As for Drake, although he'd kept his word about not mentioning Josie's visit, he hadn't kept the other part of the bargain. Thinking back on the course of events, she couldn't really blame him. She'd made the first move, and it had been a doozy.

"I knew you'd be fit to be tied if you found out I warned him off. I didn't ever plan to tell you, but now that I know Drake's probably going to be over there a lot, it's only fair you know what was said. I knew if the mare went into labor you'd call Drake. I hoped that wouldn't happen, but after listening to Jerry Rankin, I had a bad feeling that it *would.*"

Tracy had no idea what to say. Josie's worst fears had come true. She'd become involved with Drake, and maybe it would end up in a mess. But Drake had given her the courage to reach out for the passion she'd been denying herself out of fear. She cherished that he'd given her permission to be sexually adventuresome, but it wasn't the kind of thing she was ready to tell Josie.

Josie's expression was filled with compassion. "The thing is, I don't…I don't want you to get hurt."

"I appreciate that." Tracy knew her friend's motives were pure, but she'd left Tracy's shiny new view of life somewhat tarnished. Not completely, but she didn't feel as joyous as she had earlier this morning. She wished Drake hadn't assured Josie he would stay clear. But she tried to imagine how she'd have felt if he'd told her then what he'd said to Josie. What if he'd rejected her because of that?

She would have been crushed. If her first attempt at seducing a man had ended in failure, she might not have worked up the courage to try it again. Drake had been in a no-win situation. He could either honor his word to Josie or help a repressed woman break away from her self-imposed restrictions.

He'd chosen to help her. That had to be worth something. Of course he'd enjoyed himself, too, so his decision hadn't been totally unselfish.

"I should probably apologize for prying into your business," Josie said. "But I think of you as a little sister. I've known you ever since you were a kid. You've had your share of lumps, and Drake is just not… He's just not the man I would trust to make you happy. I wish he could be, but I don't think so. Not right now, anyway."

"You're probably right. He is in a transitional period, and I can see him breaking a woman's heart without ever meaning to do it. He's gorgeous and women find him irresistible." She hesitated, but there was no point in being coy. "Me included."

"I know, honey, and I don't blame you for that. He's one hot guy. All I can say is, be careful. Be very careful."

"I will." But she hadn't been at all careful so far.

Josie pushed away from the desk. "I'd better go fetch my son and let you get to work."

"Yeah." Tracy's throat felt tight.

"If there's anything I can do, let me know. If the foal's been born, then you probably don't need Drake to monitor the situation anymore. Jack could do it. He'd be glad to, in fact."

"That's very generous. I'll let you know." But inside she was loudly protesting that Drake was the man for the job. She didn't want Jack or anyone else taking care of Dottie and Sprinkles.

She and Drake should do it. They'd been there for the birth, and they were the obvious ones to handle the next few days as mother and son became stronger. All four of them had shared a bonding experience, and Tracy didn't want it to be over. Not yet.

Besides, tonight she was taking Drake out hat shopping. Buying him a hat wasn't going to miraculously give him answers for how to live his life. She knew that. But she thought it might be a start.

11

DRAKE WAS STANDING at the island in the kitchen chopping veggies for Wilbur and Harley when he heard Tracy's little white truck pull up outside. Two of his poetry journals sat on the small kitchen table. He'd gone back to the cabin for clothes, and after much inner debate, he'd brought his journals, too.

The decision hadn't been easy. Right before driving away, he'd turned off the engine, taken the journals out of the SUV and put them back in the cabin. Then he'd called himself a lily-livered coward and thrown them onto the front seat, where his duffel sat filled with clean clothes.

That had been another difficult call. He didn't know yet whether he was staying for more than one night. He'd finally decided on clothing for two days, hardly enough to make it seem he was moving in for the duration. If Tracy wanted him to stay longer, he'd run the washing machine. He hoped he'd end up doing that.

He ought to wash Regan's stuff, no matter how things worked out…or didn't.

Tonight while they were in Jackson, he'd pick up replacements for the toiletries he'd used. Tracy might decide against telling Regan and Lily that he'd slept over. He'd respect her wishes on that.

All he knew was that the sound of her truck set his blood to pumping, and when she opened the front door, he had to stop himself from going to meet her. But he had a sharp knife in one hand and a head of cauliflower in the other. He stayed where he was and kept chopping. "I'm in here!"

When she walked through the kitchen doorway, he could tell something was on her mind. He'd fantasized that she'd come over and lay one on him in greeting, but it didn't look as if that dream would come true. "Tough day?"

She managed a smile, but it lacked sparkle. "Not exactly. Let me get rid of my purse and I'll help you." She walked over to the kitchen table.

He held his breath.

"What's this? Are these your…" Her voice trailed off.

When he glanced over, she'd picked up the top journal and opened it.

"You don't have to read them now." He was sweating, and not because the room was particularly hot. "In fact, you don't have to read them at all. It was an afterthought to bring them." Then he cursed under his breath. "Actually it wasn't an afterthought. That was one of the reasons I drove back home this morning."

She glanced up, her eyes shining. "Drake, this first one is beautiful."

"I...um...thanks." Dear God, he was blushing. He could feel it.

"It's as if I'm there in the pasture with you in the early morning light, with dew on the grass, and the horses chasing each other, *their hooves tossing diamonds through sunbeams*. I love that!"

He swallowed. "This is way more embarrassin' than I thought it would be."

"Please don't be embarrassed." She closed the journal and held it against her chest. "You can't know how honored I am that you're willing to let me read what you've written. But you'll have to help me with some of it. Your handwriting is atrocious."

He chuckled and the knot of tension in his stomach eased. "Thank God for bad handwriting. This moment was just cryin' out for some comic relief."

"Bringing the journals was very brave." She walked toward him, still holding the journal close.

Holding it against her heart. Her reaction left no doubt that she understood what showing her those journals had cost him, would continue to cost him as she read through them. "I decided if you could step out of your comfort zone, then so could I."

She came right up to him, then. Still holding the book clutched against her breast, she wrapped one arm around his neck. "Lean toward me, cowboy. I want to kiss you hello."

He put down the knife and the head of cauliflower. "My hands are wet."

She smiled. "I didn't ask you to hold on to me. I'll hold on to you. Just lean down like I asked you to. Last night you put me in charge, and I've discovered I like that. A lot."

"I really have created a monster." But he rested his wet hands on the counter and bent toward her as instructed, so that his mouth was available for her hello kiss, the one he'd thought he wouldn't get.

Ah, but he got it now. She started out soft and light, but before long she'd invaded his mouth with her sassy tongue, and he'd returned the favor. When she began to suck on his tongue, his blood flowed south to the area he would love to have her suck on next.

They hadn't gotten around to that particular game last night, and from the way she was kissing him, he'd bet money she was thinking about it now. He considered wiping his hands on his jeans so he could grab hold of her and carry her down the hall. Or hoist her up on the kitchen island. It was sturdy enough.

Just when he'd lifted his damp palms from the counter to take action, she broke away and stepped back. He opened his eyes, hoping to see her put down the book and unbutton her blouse. Or put down the book so he could undress her.

Instead she continued to hold it tight against her heaving bosom. "We can't right now."

The sound of their breathing was loud in the otherwise silent kitchen. He finally did wipe his hands on his jeans. "The way I'm feeling, it wouldn't take long."

Fire burned in her dark eyes, and her moist lips were temptingly parted as she gulped in air. Then slowly her gaze lowered to his protruding fly. Her voice was pure temptation. "Promise?"

His heartbeat went from fast to rocket speed. He didn't pretend to misunderstand. He couldn't even bring himself to turn down her unspoken offer. He'd been semiaroused all day thinking about her, and one kiss had tipped the balance. He ached with a fierceness that could last a while, unless…unless he surrendered. He looked into her eyes. "Promise."

Her slow smile of anticipation was all any man could wish for. She'd not only offered. She wanted to. Setting the journal on a tall stool next to the island, she knelt in front of him and reached for his zipper. Blood sang in his ears as she drew it down. She found the opening in his briefs and freed his eager penis.

Trembling, he braced himself for the first slide of her mouth. Fast was one thing. Coming the second she began was not his idea of cool.

As she wrapped her fingers around his girth, she lifted her head and looked up at him. "You have a beautiful cock, Drake Brewster."

Once again, she'd left him speechless. That soft groan had probably come from him, though. His brain lacked a normal blood supply, so he couldn't be sure of anything.

She gave him that sultry smile again. "I look forward to paying my respects to it." With that, she dipped her head and took him in.

The woman didn't mess around. She took him deep, so deep that the sensitive tip bumped the back of her throat. He gasped and fought the urge to come. He was so glad he fought that urge, so glad he'd held on for the next part.

That first move was only the beginning of the ride. Next she used her tongue to massage the front ridge. After that she hollowed her cheeks and slid her mouth up and down in a rhythm guaranteed to make him a happy man. And all the while she used both hands to squeeze, stroke and pet him until he was delirious with pleasure.

He shoved his hands into her glossy hair and sent hairpins flying. His moans increased as she moved faster and sucked harder. At last those moans blended into one triumphant cry as he erupted. As his cock pulsed in the warm haven of her mouth, his lust-soaked brain swirled with one overarching thought—he'd never had sex this good.

She stayed with him to the end, her swallows the kind of erotic sound men dream of. Shuddering with the force of his orgasm, he gripped the edge of the kitchen island for support.

Gently she rearranged his briefs and carefully pulled the zipper back in place. "There."

His laugh was more of a croak, but he mentally saluted her for getting in one more cheeky comment relating to their joke from last night. Besides being an enthusiastic lover, she was just plain fun. When he'd first met her at the Spirits and Spurs, he hadn't guessed that. Then again, she'd disapproved of him. Judging from what had just happened, she no longer did.

He recovered enough to help her to her feet. "You're incredible."

"You inspire me." She picked up his journal and held it as before, pressed against her heart.

He met her gaze. "If my poetry affects you that way, I'll devote my life to it."

"Let's put it this way—your poems didn't hurt your cause any. Women are suckers for a poetry-writing man. I'm surprised you've never shown it to other women."

"Maybe I should have trusted them more, but I didn't."

She studied him for several seconds. "Why me?"

"I've asked myself the same thing." He cupped her face in both hands and looked into the unexplored depths of those beautiful eyes. "For some reason I feel safe with you. I didn't expect I ever would, especially after our blowup at the dinner table. But you explained why that happened, and then…then you put yourself out there, took the risk." He smiled. "I guess you could say you put your money where your mouth is. Not everyone has the guts to do that."

She wrapped her arms around his waist. "I didn't used to. You came along at the perfect time, when I was ready to grow. You sprinkled on some fertilizer, and I blossomed."

He grinned. "Are you telling me I'm full of shit?"

"Yeah." She laughed and gave him a squeeze. "And that was exactly what I needed, apparently. So what do you say? Ready to finish feeding the critters and go buy a hat?"

"If I wasn't before, I am now. If I'm worthy of what you just did, I'm sure as hell worthy of a hat."

"Excellent. Then let's get to it."

Less than an hour later, they'd fed everyone and made sure Dottie and Sprinkles were progressing as expected. Tracy had fixed the hair arrangement he'd destroyed and settled into the passenger seat of his SUV.

She'd wanted to bring one of his journals for the road, but he'd talked her out of it. He couldn't handle having her read snippets of his work to him while they sailed down the highway. And she would have. He'd already figured that out.

When they were finally headed toward Jackson, she leaned back into the leather seat, anticipation glowing in her eyes. "If you want, we can grab something quick for dinner before we look for hats."

He set the SUV on cruise control. The sun was low on the horizon and traffic was light. Easy trip. "I do want food at some point. A really good orgasm makes a man hungry, and you, ma'am, gave me a really good orgasm."

"Glad to hear it. You probably won't believe this, but I've never initiated something like that. I'd do it if a guy asked me, but I wasn't bold enough to suggest it on my own, especially in a kitchen."

He couldn't resist teasing her. "How about in a dining room? Is that any better?" She started to laugh, and he kept going. "What about the laundry room? Or the hallway? I personally think a blow job in the hallway would be—"

"Stop!" She punched him playfully on the arm. "I just meant that I've never had oral sex anywhere except in a bedroom."

"Are you talking about you doing it to him or him doing it to you?"

"Both. Either. Only in bedrooms."

"We have to remedy *that*. I didn't realize last night was a damned cliché."

"Trust me, it wasn't."

"You're sure?" He shot her another look and discovered that her cheeks were pink. "I mean, we were in a bed, so how special could it be for you? Been there, done that."

"Not with such…finesse."

"Ah." He liked the sound of that.

"Or concentration. I've never come twice in a row during oral sex."

"Then maybe it wasn't such a cliché after all."

"You're fishing for compliments!"

He shook his head, although he totally was. With great effort he managed not to laugh. "I just don't want to be redundant."

"You are absolutely fishing, but I don't mind telling you that the oral sex with you is the best I've ever had."

Now that was enough to make a man's chest puff out, for sure. "I'm glad to hear that. I—"

"And now that I've stroked your male ego, it's—"

"Stroked my ego? Do you mean you were lying?"

"Not at all. You rocked my world in a way no man ever has, but if you can fish for compliments, so can I. How would you rate my blow job?"

He almost drove off the road. "*Rate? What do you mean, rate?*"

"On a scale of one to ten. Obviously you've had much

more experience than I have, so I don't expect you to score me at the top. I can put you at the top of my chart, because, to be honest, you don't have much competition."

"So I'm in a race with losers?"

"Not losers. Just men who were unimaginative in bed, and like me, probably didn't have a lot of experience. Since you've had plenty of experience, I'd be curious how I did with that episode in the kitchen."

The discussion was making him cranky. "First of all, you make me sound as if I've had dozens of women, which I haven't."

"Okay, how many?"

"A gentleman doesn't discuss specifics with a lady."

"Ballpark figure, then. More or less than twenty?"

"I'm not answering that." Because he couldn't. He'd have to sort through his entire sexual history, which would take some time. But he was afraid it was more than twenty, and that…sounded like a man who had superficial affairs.

At this moment, he didn't want to confirm what Tracy probably already suspected. He'd never had a serious relationship. Not ever.

"I'll assume it's more than twenty," she said, "because if it had been less, you would have said so. Okay, forget about the count. Let's get back to rating my performance in the kitchen. You can tell me the truth. As I said, I don't expect to outrank everyone. I'm too inexperienced for that."

"Damn it, it's not a sport."

"You're afraid to hurt my feelings. Really, you won't."

Just the opposite, he thought. He was afraid to tell her how strongly she affected him, for fear she'd make assumptions about a future that was unclear to him.

He began by hedging. "If I tell you the truth, I don't want you to put too much importance on it."

"Was I that terrible?"

"No," he said quietly. "You were that wonderful."

She was quiet for several seconds. "Thank you for telling me. That's nice to know."

"Tracy, I'm at a very uncertain point in my life. You're the best thing that's ever happened to me. You're an exciting lover, someone I trust with my deepest secrets, and you make me laugh more than anyone I know. You're perfect. But I may not be ready for you."

Another long silence. "That's pretty close to what Josie said today."

"Josie? You talked to her?" He envisioned their current discussion going quickly downhill. Maybe this was why she'd come home looking frazzled. Finding his journal had caught her attention, and the sexual chemistry between them had distracted her even more. But now they were getting down to it. "What did she say?"

"Kind of what you said, that you don't have a clue what you'll end up doing with your life, and that a person in your position isn't ready for a relationship with someone like me."

"Josie's a very smart lady. You should probably listen to her."

"I found out she asked you to stay away from me, and you told her you'd already decided to do that."

He stared at the road ahead. "That was the plan. Then you showed up in a red silk bathrobe and boots."

"I know, and I don't blame you for going back on your promise to Josie. But she knows about the mare and foal now. She pointed out that Jack could probably handle them from here on out. You're under no obligation to stay if you think it would be easier on you if you left."

His jaw tightened. "Not easier on me. Probably easier on you, though."

"So you're ready to make that decision for me, just like Josie?"

"Tracy, you're rooted to this place. I'm not. I worry about how it will affect you if I end up leaving, after all."

"Well, don't worry about that! Just don't!"

He glanced at her in surprise. "I can't help it. I care about you."

"I understand that. But you have to try." She sounded resolute. "You and Josie have to quit worrying about how I'll survive if you and I don't work out. Let me worry about that, okay?"

"But—"

"I'm serious, Drake. You're the most exciting man I've ever met. If I want to enjoy every possible minute with you, if I want to say damn the torpedoes, full speed ahead, that's my privilege."

He thought about that. "I guess it is."

"It sure as hell is. I want you to stay at Peaceful Kingdom until Regan and Lily come home. If you're still here at that point, I'm inviting you to share my apartment, which, to answer the question in your note, is above Spirits and Spurs."

His brain was still spinning from her unexpected determination to carry on, no matter what. But he managed an appropriate response. "That sounds cozy."

"It is. However, if we don't get that far, then please know that I'll be fine. I'll be grateful for what we've shared, and I won't wail and gnash my teeth when you leave."

He risked another quick glance at her face, to see if he saw any humor there. He did, so he decided to nourish it. "Not even a little wailing and gnashing?"

"Oh, all right. A little bit. After all, I'll miss the sex."

"Yeah. Me, too." He reached over and took her hand. "Me, too." He'd love to think that they'd ease into a lasting relationship, but in his present situation, that seemed so unlikely. Yet she'd told him exactly what she wanted from him—as much fun as he could provide until it was time to leave. He'd do that for her. But he'd still worry.

12

TRACY SUGGESTED A little hamburger joint she'd tried on her last trip to Jackson, because for the rest of the week they'd be eating vegetarian meals.

"You could also come into the bar when I'm working during the dinner hour this week," Tracy said as they finished their burgers and sipped the rest of their draft beer. "I'll serve you up a juicy hamburger even better than this, and this was darned good."

"It was."

"Thank you for buying me dinner, Drake." He'd already paid the bill, but neither of them had made a move to leave. Sitting and talking had been nice.

"It's been my pleasure, ma'am." He picked up his remaining pub fry. "When's your next evening shift?"

"Tomorrow night. Maybe you should come in."

He chewed slowly. "Depends on whether you think Josie will be there. Did you tell her I'm staying at Peaceful Kingdom?"

"No. I should have." She felt like a wuss for listening to all of Josie's warnings without admitting they were superfluous now. The horse was out of the barn, so to speak.

"You don't have to if you'd rather not. It's really none of her business."

"She said that, too, but I'm not sure she believes it. Josie's protective of the people she loves."

"Nothing wrong with that." He shoved back his empty plate. "As long as we're getting this all out on the table, I'll tell you that Regan was convinced you and I would get together while they were gone."

"Why would he assume that?"

"I admitted that I thought you were hot."

"You did?" She flushed with pleasure. "I didn't realize that. You never really flirted with me."

"Tracy, I never flirted with *anybody* in Shoshone. When you're the guy who seduced his best friend's fiancée, and you're in that guy's hometown, you don't flirt. Period."

"Come on. It hasn't been *that* bad."

"Wanna bet? Husbands would give me the stink eye if I so much as glanced in the direction of their wives. I gave up looking at women, at least most of the time. I still watched you behind the bar when I thought nobody was payin' attention."

"I watched you, too."

"Yeah?" He looked pleased. "And here I thought you hated my guts." He polished off his beer.

"I tried to, but the minute I laid eyes on you, I got all hot and bothered. I started taking more time with my hair and makeup before going in to work, in case you'd show up at the bar."

"All I can say is, you always looked great. You were a bright spot in my life, even if I didn't think I had a chance with you."

"And see what's happened."

He reached over and laced his fingers through hers. "I'm a lucky guy. Thanks for givin' me that chance."

"Glad I did." Tracy gazed at him across the checkered tablecloth and finally found the courage to ask the question that mattered the most, in her mind, at least. "Did you love her?"

He blinked. "Love who?" The confusion in his expression slowly cleared. "Oh. You mean Jeannette."

"Yes."

"It's not an easy question to answer."

"Then never mind," Tracy said quickly. "You don't have to answer it now. You don't ever have to answer it."

"But you want to know."

She couldn't lie. "Yes."

"Because if I secretly loved her all along, that makes what I did a little easier to swallow, right?" He caressed her palm with his thumb.

She wondered if he even realized he was doing it. He was a naturally sensual man who enjoyed touching people. She'd benefited greatly from that. Now she wished she hadn't brought up Jeannette, but she'd started the discussion, so she couldn't drop it now. "If you loved her, what happened would be more understandable, I guess."

"Yes, I loved Jeannette. Still do."

It was the answer that would help absolve him, so why did it hurt so much when he said it? Tracy reminded herself that she'd asked, and she didn't want him to lie, so if she didn't like the answer, too bad. She started to pull her hand away.

He tightened his grip and held on. "Tracy, don't. Let me explain. I've known Jeannette since we were kids. We've been buddies. I never dated her. We went to the University of Virginia, and that's where I met Regan. He and I got along great, so of course I introduced him to my pal Jeannette. They sort of drifted into a relationship."

Tracy's mood improved, but she still wondered if Drake was a little bit in love with his childhood friend. "That doesn't sound very romantic."

"It didn't seem like it to me, either, but they both insisted they were blissfully happy. They had it all— great careers, promising future, yada yada yada. Regan loves being a vet, no matter what the circumstances. I liked it okay, but I never loved the job the way he does, maybe because it was my parents' idea. They always wanted me to open a practice specializing in thorough-bred racehorses. They were paying the bills, and I took the path of least resistance."

She suspected he'd been under way more pressure than he was letting on. Although she could be wrong, she had a feeling his entire life had been laid out for him, and he'd been expected to follow the yellow brick road, no questions asked. "Were you writing, then?"

"Oh, sure, but I wasn't going to make a living writing poetry, especially if I never told anybody I was doin' it."

"Well, there's that. But you're right. Most poets have day jobs."

"I know, and I thought being a vet could be my day job. But I wasn't just an equine vet. I was a vet for animals worth millions. I thought I'd be thrilled with the prestige, but I wasn't. I hated the pressure."

Because you're a poet. "But not Regan?"

"He's like Teflon. It just rolled off of him. He has this inner core of certainty, no matter what he does. I envied how he had everything goin' his way when I so obviously didn't have a clue. Instead of trying to get my act together, which looked impossible, I threw a rock into the calm pool of his perfect life, because that was easy."

She gazed at him in admiration. "But Drake, you figured out why you did it. Most people aren't willing to do that. And you've made amends. On top of everything else, Regan's life wasn't as perfect as it looked. If you hadn't thrown that rock, he wouldn't be here. He wouldn't have found Lily and Peaceful Kingdom. He loves her and he loves that place."

"True, and I feel a little better when I think about that. But I can't say Jeannette and I are friends anymore. I tried to justify what we did by continuing to see her, but neither of us could get past the guilt. We ended the affair, but our friendship died with it. What a waste."

"Have you contacted her since you came out here?" Tracy had to ask. He'd rebuilt the friendship with Regan, and he could do the same with Jeannette. Once the guilt was gone, maybe they'd discover they really did love each other. That made her stomach clench, but she'd be incredibly selfish not to suggest that he try to repair his relationship with a woman he'd known for years.

"I haven't contacted her, but that's a good idea. Maybe I could get her to come out here for a few days. She could talk to Regan, then, too. I'd ask him, first, though, before I asked her to come."

"Definitely. I think Lily would be okay with it. She's all about mending fences, but still. Jeannette was his fiancée. You don't want to put Lily in an awkward position." *Or me.* But she had no claim to Drake and no right to feel jealous of Jeannette. If the thought of Jeannette showing up in Jackson Hole made her feel sick to her stomach, she'd have to get over it.

"Thanks for the suggestion." Drake smiled and squeezed her hand again. "Have I told you how great you are?"

"Maybe not when we have all our clothes on."

"Then let me say it now, when we're fully dressed and sitting in a public place where there's no chance we'll be getting naked anytime soon. You're terrific. You—"

"Miss Tracy, Miss Tracy!"

Tracy yanked her hand free and turned toward the little redhead racing toward her. Sarah Bianca Chance, aka SB, was in the restaurant. Because she was only three, she undoubtedly hadn't arrived alone.

SB threw herself into Tracy's arms. "Guess what? Me, Mommy and Daddy saw a movie! Not my brother. He's too little. We didn't get popcorn but we're gonna get *hamburgers*." Then she turned to stare at Drake. "Who's that?"

"That's Mr. Drake, SB." A very pregnant Morgan Chance, her red hair a shade darker than her daughter's, walked up to the table followed by her husband, Gabe. "Hi, Trace. Nice to see you." Morgan's voice was cool and her expression remained carefully neutral.

That alone told Tracy how upset she must be, because Morgan's face was always animated and her blue-green eyes constantly sparkled with delight. She didn't look the least bit delighted now. She'd probably seen Drake and Tracy holding hands, too. Tracy was afraid she'd just been branded a traitor.

Drake got to his feet immediately and held out his hand to Morgan. "I'm honored to finally meet one of Regan's sisters."

Morgan shook his hand, but she made it brief. "This is my husband, Gabe."

Gabe stepped forward, and he wasn't smiling, either. "Brewster." He shook Drake's hand with a little more force than necessary. Then he moved back, smoothed two fingers over his sandy mustache and glanced around the restaurant as if desperately searching for an appropriate comment. "Kind of crowded tonight."

"It is." Tracy stood, too. "But we're about to leave if you want this table."

"That's okay," Morgan said. "I like to be by the window. Gabe, would you please go ask the hostess to put us on the list for a window table? And take SB with you?"

"Sure thing." Gabe looked relieved as he held out his hand to SB. "Come on, peanut. We need to ask her about crayons."

"Right!" The little girl hopped up and down. "I want

to color!" She hurried over to her father and skipped along by his side.

Morgan watched them leave before turning back to Tracy. "Well, this is awkward. I didn't know you two were…seeing each other."

"It's a long story," Tracy said. "I took in a pregnant mare yesterday and she delivered last night, so rather than pay for a vet, I asked Drake to come over. Regan said I should call on him in an emergency."

"I vaguely remember hearing about that, but…" She glanced from Tracy to Drake. "This doesn't look like a veterinary emergency. It looks like a date."

"Tracy's been workin' hard," Drake said. "I thought she could use a little break, so we—"

"He's staying with me at Peaceful Kingdom." Tracy looked Morgan squarely in the eye. "There's no point in trying to hide it. And he's not there just because of the mare and foal, although I appreciate the huge help he's been. We've discovered we really like each other."

Morgan nodded. "Okay, then." She gazed at both of them for a moment longer. "I'd better go find Gabe and SB. You two have a nice night." She still didn't smile.

Neither did Drake, but he'd been raised to be a gentleman, so Tracy wasn't surprised when he responded with his typical *thank you, ma'am*. If he'd had a hat on, he could have touched its brim as another gesture of respect. Now more than ever she wanted him to have that hat. If he had to put up with being snubbed, at least he could walk proudly and wear a big hat.

She stood beside him as Morgan walked away. "Sorry about that. I should have remembered that Morgan and Gabe like this place, too, but I still can't believe they showed up tonight, and while we were here, too! Another ten minutes and we would have been gone."

Drake glanced down at her, warm concern in his gaze. "I'm not the least bit sorry about it for my sake. But you just announced to the world that we're sleepin' together. I'm honored that you did, but you blew me away, sayin' that."

"Folks might assume it, anyway, once Morgan reports that we were eating a meal together and holding hands."

"Because of my reputation." He scowled. "You're probably right, damn it."

"Frankly, I'm relieved we don't have to sneak around. I'd rather take the offensive and get it out in the open instead of having people talk behind our backs. Now, shall we go? Or do you want to stand here and give me a big old kiss in front of everybody?"

He grinned at her. "While that has enormous appeal, if we're going to make that dramatic gesture, we should do it somewhere more fittin', like in the middle of Shoshone's main street."

"I like that idea! Save it for later. For now, we need to go get you a hat." She took his hand. "We'll pass them again on our way to the door. Break out that fabulous smile of yours."

"I will if you will."

"You've got it, cowboy." Her fingers firmly laced through his, she walked with her back straight and her head high. When they reached the cluster of diners waiting for tables, she beamed at Morgan, Gabe and SB. "Great to see you!"

"It's been a real pleasure." Drake's voice oozed Southern charm.

At first Morgan had watched them approach with cold disdain, but after they'd greeted her warmly, something shifted in her expression. Unless Tracy was mistaken, Morgan's blue-green eyes now reflected a new emotion—grudging respect.

"That was entertainin'." Drake continued to hold her hand as they strolled around the Jackson town square toward the Western wear store. "I don't imagine we'll have nearly as much fun in the store."

"You might be surprised."

"How so?"

"I predict you'll go in a Southern gentleman and you'll come out a cowboy."

"They'll teach me to rope in there, too? Now that's a bargain."

"They won't teach you to rope, but once you have a hat, you'll look like you can rope. Then you'll be more motivated to learn to rope so you'll match your hat."

Drake laughed. "That's way too complicated for this Southern boy. I may not be ready for this hat, after all."

She hoped he was only kidding. "Don't wimp out on me now, Brewster."

"I won't." He released her hand and wrapped an arm around her shoulders as they approached the store with its windows full of mannequins wearing Western outfits. "I've seen the light. Any man lucky enough to be sharin' a bed with you had better own a decent hat." He reached out and opened the glass door for her.

She smiled at him as she walked past. "Or an indecent one."

"Better watch out, sweetheart. You're playin' with fire."

"I surely hope so." Catching his hand, she led him over to the shelves filled with Western hats. "What strikes your fancy?"

He took his time looking over the display. "It needs to be black."

"I hope that doesn't have anything to do with your story about white hats and black hats." She was only half teasing.

"No, it doesn't." He picked up a black Stetson by the brim. "Much as I loved those movies, white hats make no sense. They'll just get dirty."

"And they don't look nearly as sexy as black."

He smiled at her. "Lord knows I want to look sexy for you." And he put on the hat.

Tracy caught her breath. Whether by accident or instinct, he'd chosen the perfect hat. He'd also managed to put it on at exactly the right angle. The brim shadowed his eyes just enough to make him look even more manly, if that was even possible.

He gazed at her from under that brim. "Is that sexy enough for you?"

She swallowed. "I think…it might be overkill."

13

ILLOGICAL THOUGH IT might be, Drake felt different wearing the hat. He'd never have bought it without Tracy's urging, without her belief in him. She'd given him a renewed faith in his essential decency, and then she'd made the hat into a symbol, one he could relate to. One he could wear, for God's sake. How great was that? He owed her, big-time.

Wearing it out of that store, he wasn't convinced that he'd been magically transformed into a cowboy. That would be delusional. But he did feel like a better man.

He might never learn how to twirl a rope, but he would live up to what the hat stood for. He would never again attempt to ease his own pain by causing pain to those he loved. He was better than that.

Tracy kept staring at him, so he was pretty sure the hat was working for her, too. He took hold of her hand again as they stood on the sidewalk outside the store. "Anything else you want to do while we're in town, little lady?"

She laughed, which made her eyes light up and her cheeks rosy. "Just because you have a hat doesn't mean you have to talk like John Wayne."

He loved seeing her like that, so he continued the riff. "Oh, I think it does. And look. Now I'm bowlegged." He managed a pigeon-toed stance that was fairly convincing. "I'm also hankerin' for a cold sarsaparilla and a tin plate full of beans."

"Stop, just stop!"

But she was still bubbling over with laughter, so of course he didn't stop. "If I could find me a nice long piece of straw, I do believe I'd chew on it."

Giggling, she shook her head. "You're ridiculous."

"And here I thought the hat was supposed to make me sexy. Maybe I should return it and get my money back." He started to take it off.

"Don't you dare remove that hat, cowboy, or I'll have to hurt you."

"Whoa!" He crammed it back on his head so the brim made his ears stick out. "I sure hope you're not packin', little lady, or I might have to vamoose."

Grinning, she stepped back and surveyed him. "You have totally screwed up your sexy, but I think it's salvageable. Come here and lean down. Let me fix you."

He did as she asked because he had to agree there was way too much space between them.

Lifting the hat slightly, she set it back on his head more as he'd had it the first time. "There."

"I like it when you say that word." He straightened. "It makes me think of you...naked." He cupped the back of her head. "I might have to kiss you in the middle of Jackson instead of waiting until we get to Shoshone."

"I'm not sure that's a good idea."

"Why? Is there a law against it around here?"

"No, but—"

"Then let's do it." But the minute he started the maneuver, he understood the problem. Damned if his hat wasn't in the way. He angled his head one way, then the other. "How the hell can I do this without poking your eye out?"

"Nudge it back like this." Tracy reached up and pushed it slightly back on his forehead.

"Ah." Simple and elegant. He could finally achieve the desired connection with her smiling mouth. As always, making that connection felt like coming home. He settled in with a sigh. It wouldn't be a long kiss, just enough to hold him until they got back to the house.

She wound her arms around his neck and pressed against him with a carefully controlled passion that matched his own. It was an open-mouthed kiss with a restrained use of tongues, a PG-13 kind of kiss suitable for a public street corner. But any kiss involving Tracy could swing into X-rated territory if he didn't watch himself. He ended it before he forgot where he was and embarrassed them both.

Drawing back, he smiled down at her. "Nice."

"Yeah." She reached up and pulled his hat back where it had been. "Now take me home, cowboy. I want to have my way with you."

He didn't need more motivation than that. They were back in the SUV and on the road in no time. He started to take his hat off, because it seemed silly to keep it on for the drive home.

She put a hand on his arm, stopping him. "Leave it on. For me."

He settled it back on his head.

"Do you like it?" she asked. "I hope you do, because it wasn't cheap."

"Yeah, I do like it. A lot." He glanced over at her. "Thank you for talkin' me into it."

"You're welcome."

He returned his attention to the road, but from the corner of his eye he could see that she was staring at him. "Are you fixated on my hat?"

"A little. But I'm also thinking about what you said tonight at dinner, about not loving your job, although you do seem to like working with horses."

"Apparently I like it fine when the horses aren't valuable thoroughbreds. I had fun supervising Dottie's foaling."

"So did I." Her voice rippled with amusement.

"I wasn't talking about the sex!"

"I know. Sorry. Couldn't resist. So you had fun supervising the foaling."

"I did. I was working with a beautiful, but essentially ordinary, horse. Dottie's not going to run in the Derby. Neither is Sprinkles. I finally recognized that night that I *do* want horses in my life, just not under the conditions I had before. I also like the idea that we were there for Dottie when she had nowhere else to go."

"So you like the rescue angle?"

"It's brilliant. I hope the computer game Lily developed continues to pay those nice royalties so she can afford to keep Peaceful Kingdom goin' forever."

"So do I, but even if the royalties dry up, she'll find another way to pay for it. She'll organize fund-raisers of some kind or look for wealthy investors. She's committed to the horses. So's Regan."

Drake nodded. "You're right. She'll move heaven and earth if she has to."

"You could do that, too."

He looked at her in confusion. "Help her raise money? I suppose I could."

"No, I mean raise money for your own rescue operation. You're a charmer, Drake. You'd be great at running a horse-adoption facility. Fund-raising would be a snap for someone with your personality."

The suggestion caught him completely by surprise. "I don't... Wow, I'd never thought about *me* doin' it."

"Think about it. You'd be a natural."

Slowly the possibility took hold of his imagination. "I was planning to sell my share of the practice, anyway. I could use that as seed money, maybe a down payment on a location."

"There you go."

His brain clicked into high gear. "You know where something like that is needed?"

"Everywhere."

"That's true, but I was thinking of Virginia. Racehorses are worth a ton of money until they're not. There may already be equine rescues for racing thoroughbreds, but it's a big industry. They could probably use another one."

"And you already have the vet skills. You wouldn't have to worry about getting a volunteer for that."

"No, and thanks to my practice, I have a network of wealthy people who might be looking for a tax credit or a write-off. Tracy, this might actually work." Excitement fizzed in his veins until he realized the big drawback to his plan. She wouldn't be part of it.

Not that she couldn't be, but he couldn't ask her to leave this town and the people who had practically raised her. Shoshone already had an equine-adoption facility. The town was small and didn't need another one. Nick and Regan had the vet situation covered, and all they might require in the future was a part-time employee, somebody like Jerry Rankin.

"You're quiet over there."

"Just thinkin'."

"If you don't mind thinking out loud, I'd love hearing whatever plans you're cooking up for this new place. It'll be wonderful, Drake. You might even have time to do some writing on the side."

"I might." He decided to test her reaction to an alternative. "I wonder if maybe I should consider a different location, something closer to this area."

"Why? All your connections are back there, and you know thoroughbreds so well. You're uniquely qualified to set up a rescue and adoption facility for racehorses."

He knew he was on shaky ground, but he'd give it a shot. "You thought this up. It seems like you should be involved, somehow."

She was silent for quite a while.

"Tracy? You okay over there?"

"Yes."

"Look, I realize we haven't known each other very long, but speaking strictly for myself, I'd like to see where this relationship might go. If I head off to Virginia, we won't get that chance."

Her voice was soft, but filled with sincerity. "You shouldn't base your decision on me."

"But—"

"Seriously, Drake." Her voice grew stronger. "You haven't said it in so many words, but I get the impression you've been doing what other people want for a long time. You should do what's best for you now."

"What if being with you is what's best for me? You need to be here. I get it. So if I choose to work around your needs, what's so terrible about that?"

"I'm not sure I can explain, but it doesn't feel right to me. It feels as if you're contorting your plans to fit mine instead of going straight toward your goal."

"Hell, I wouldn't even have a goal if you hadn't suggested it!" The truth was, he wanted everything. He could envision the rescue operation in Virginia perfectly. She was right that it suited him right down to the ground. But he wanted to spend more time with her and find out if they had the kind of special something that would take them through the next fifty years. He thought they might.

Yet she was the town sweetheart, rooted firmly in this community, watched over by the likes of Josie and Jack Chance. She'd told him how much she loved it here, so coaxing her to move back east would be extremely selfish.

He might be able to do it because she liked him and she liked the sex. She might think that would make up for all she'd lose by leaving here. But it would be like yanking a beautiful wildflower out of the ground and then wondering why it wilted and died.

He had to think about this some more. He didn't want to ruin the time they had together at Peaceful Kingdom by arguing about it, either. "It's a great idea," he said at last. "I want to mull it over for a while before making any firm decisions."

"Would you care to translate that? It sounds like doublespeak."

He chuckled. She wouldn't let him get away with anything, which was one of her traits he cherished the most. "Okay. I love havin' sex with you and we have the house to ourselves for at least another five nights. Let's not mess that up with deep, philosophical discussions about the future. Let's live for the present."

She didn't answer right away, but eventually she did. "Okay."

"Excellent."

"I want you to leave your hat on."

"I am leaving it on. I have it on right this minute per your specific request."

"I mean leave it on after you've taken everything else off."

He laughed. "So when we get home, you want me naked except for my hat?"

"That's what I'm saying. You were turned on by my boots. I'm turned on by your hat."

"Fair enough."

"So you'll do it?"

"I'll do it, although I can't picture how it will work."

"That's okay. I can."

TRACY HAD A very clear picture of what she wanted, and she kept it firmly in mind as they drove the rest of the way home. They talked about Dottie and Sprinkles. She told him that Josie had suggested Jack could take over from this point, but she was prepared to tell Josie that wouldn't be necessary. She'd call her boss in the morning.

But even as she said that, she knew Josie wouldn't need a call. She had Morgan, who might have already spread the word that Tracy was sleeping with none other than the evil Drake Brewster. Josie might not like hearing the news, but at least she wouldn't have the kind of fit Morgan might have expected.

They talked about Dottie and Sprinkles for the rest of the trip. Drake wanted to let both of them out into the pasture tomorrow with some supervision, and he expected the new foal's first outing to go fine. Tracy wished she had a proper video camera instead of just her phone, but she'd make do.

While she kept up her end of the conversation, she hadn't stopped thinking about Drake's equine rescue in Virginia. Establishing it there had been his instinctive response, and it was the right one. That first poem of his told her how much he loved his native state, even if he hadn't loved his life there.

He needed to go back and create a different life, maybe even with Jeannette. Accepting that he would not stay here wasn't easy. It hurt like hell. But she wouldn't let his infatuation with her ruin what could be an exciting future.

She was convinced it was only infatuation, or perhaps even transference, a term she'd learned today while she caught up on her psych coursework during breaks at Spirits and Spurs. He wasn't a client by any stretch. If he had been, then having sex with him would have been highly unprofessional.

But she had urged him to talk about his problems, and he'd gained insight into his issues. That kind of intimate discussion, she'd learned, could cause people to imagine they'd fallen for the therapist. That might explain why Drake couldn't imagine going to Virginia without her.

She, on the other hand, had no such excuse. She was head over heels for the guy. Though it had happened quickly, she'd talked with enough women in this town to know that when lightning struck, time was irrelevant.

She was in love, but she'd never tell him. Instead she'd do everything in her power to guarantee his future happiness. Unfortunately for her, that meant encouraging him to leave.

Knowing the likely outcome of this brief affair made every minute bittersweet, but she didn't want him to know that, either. She'd keep it light and fun. That was the gift they would give to each other, and she wanted him to have good memories. As would she. The best memories ever.

After they pulled into the front yard, she let Drake help her out of the SUV because the poor guy felt guilty if he didn't perform those courtesies for a woman. They walked hand in hand down to the barn so they could assure themselves that Dottie and Sprinkles were fine.

They were. Once again they were curled up together fast asleep.

Drake put his arm around Tracy's shoulders as they watched the mare and foal. "Is it just me, or is this like when the parents come home from a night out and go check on the kids?"

"It does feel like that, doesn't it?" Her heart ached a little knowing that wasn't in the cards for them, but then, she'd never really thought it would be.

"Well, the kids are fine. Let's go." Squeezing her shoulder, he released her and held her hand as they walked out of the barn and latched the door behind them.

As they started back to the house, Tracy glanced up at the moon, which was a smidgen fuller tonight. "It was about this same time when I walked down here in my silk robe and boots."

"Are you saying it's only been twenty-four hours since then?"

"Yep." Their boots crunched on the bare dirt.

"Hard to believe. I feel as if I've known you forever."

"I know what you mean." In her case, she'd been waiting for him forever. He was the man destined to set her free from her mother's rigid rules. Whatever happened, she'd have that to remember him by. Maybe another lover as exciting as Drake would come along. She doubted it, but a miracle might happen.

"I'll never forget how you looked clutching that blanket."

"I was grateful for something to hold on to. I was shaking like a leaf."

"I wasn't all that steady, myself."

"Really?" He was so completely male and self-assured, especially wearing his new hat. "After all the experience you've had?"

"I wish you'd quit referring to that. It's not important."

"Of course it is! Practice makes perfect."

With a soft growl of frustration, he grabbed her and swung her around to face him. "Then how do you explain that when you make love with me, you are absolutely perfect? No one's ever satisfied me more than you do."

She was gratified to hear it, although she couldn't quite believe it was true. "Maybe you're easily satisfied."

He blew out an impatient breath. "It's the exact opposite. That's why my relationships usually last a few months, at most. I've never been engaged. Never seriously thought about it."

"There could be a lot of reasons for that." Her textbooks would probably list at least ten.

"Or maybe there's only one reason. Maybe nobody's ever been right for me and I'm not right for them. Maybe when two people *are* right for each other, it doesn't matter a damn bit whether they're experienced or not. They're operating from an instinct older than history, and when they come together, it's magic."

She gazed up at him. She wanted to memorize this moment when a gorgeous cowboy with the soul of a poet spoke to her of magic while stars sparkled in the sky above him and a crescent moon hung golden with promise.

He could be trying to convince himself that she was special because he needed that right now. She'd learned enough about psychology to understand that and not get her hopes up. But if she thought she'd find another man like this, she was kidding herself.

"You're magic," she murmured. "I love being with you, Drake Brewster."

"Good." He tipped back his hat as if he'd been doing it all his life. "Then let's keep it that way." This time his kiss wasn't quite so sweet or quite so restrained.

14

DRAKE KISSED TRACY until she melted like butter and they very nearly had sex in the yard. But he wasn't willing to lie in the dirt no matter how much he wanted her—and he didn't have condoms with him, either.

Getting into the house and down the hall to his bedroom was a challenge because they couldn't stop kissing and working each other out of their clothes. Well, except for his hat. It fell off three times, and Tracy always retrieved it and placed it back on his head.

They left a trail of clothes through the house and flung away the last of them as they stumbled through the door into his room. Thank God he'd left a light on, which kept them from running into the furniture. Drake grabbed a condom from the open box because he expected they'd dive straight into bed, but Tracy had other ideas.

She whirled out of his arms and stood there panting. "Hold still for a minute."

"Why?" He already had the packet and the condom in his hand, ready for action.

She gulped in air. "I want to…look at…my naked cowboy."

He was having trouble breathing, too, and he didn't want to stand around when they could be doing something more interesting. "You've seen me naked before."

"Not when you're wearing a hat." She edged toward the bed. "Stay right there. Let me get in first."

He groaned. "Tracy…"

"Humor me."

Of course he would. She could ask him to stand on his head and twirl that hat with his toes and he'd do it, or try his damnedest, because…well, because he was in love with her. Might as well face the fact.

He'd imagined himself to be in love a few times, but those relationships hadn't been anything like this—a mixture of tenderness, deep connection, wild sex and hilarity. He never wanted it to end. Impossible though it seemed, it appeared that Tracy was his first love.

But right now she was frustrating the hell out of him. His pride and joy ached something fierce, but she had a fantasy in her head that meant delaying the action. He should be rejoicing that he was part of her fantasy, but right now, all he wanted was to—

"Okay." She stretched out on the bed and propped up her head with a couple of pillows. "Pull your hat down a little lower. Perfect. You look like one badass cowboy."

"One very aroused cowboy."

"I can see that." Her gaze flicked to his johnson. "Nice."

"I could hang my hat on it."

Her lips twitched. "Don't do that. Leave your hat on and crawl toward me from the foot of the bed."

"Do you want to give me dialogue to go along with this performance, or should I make something up?"

"Make it up. Just don't call me *little lady*."

He had no idea what a badass cowboy would say in a situation like this. In the movies he'd loved as a kid, the cowboys never even kissed the women they loved, let alone talked sexy while naked except for a hat. But he'd give it his best shot.

He looked into her eyes. Telling her he loved her would probably freak her out. So instead he'd concentrate on bringing the heat.

Keeping a firm hold on the condom, he braced his other hand on the bottom edge of the mattress. Then he let his gaze travel over her body with deliberate intent. She was already trembling and flushed with anticipation, but his intimate survey stepped up the pace of her breathing. Good. It certainly stepped up the pace of his.

He pitched his voice low. "You're right accommodatin', sweetheart." He rolled the condom on one-handed. Experience counted for something, after all. "It's not every day a man finds a juicy woman without a stitch on lyin' in his bed just waitin' for it." Sliding forward, he rested one knee on the bed. "And I'm here to give you what you want, darlin'."

She swallowed. "Good."

"Oh, it will be good. Very good. I can promise you that." He moved closer and put his other knee on the bed. "I'm gonna give it to you till you can't see straight."

"I'll bet you will, cowboy." Her eyes darkened.

"And then you'll beg for more."

"Mmm." Her breasts quivered with each ragged breath.

"Now spread those pretty legs, darlin'. I'm coming in."

With a soft moan of surrender, she parted her silky thighs.

Holding her gaze, he eased into position, his cock brushing her soft folds, probing gently. Ah, so slick. So hot. She clutched his hips, her fingertips pressing, urging him forward.

He resisted, ramping up the tension, making them both want it even more. By now he knew not to mess with the hat, even though it meant he couldn't lean down and kiss her. She didn't want his kiss right now. She wanted to be taken by a cowboy.

"I think you're ready for me, sweetheart." He held himself very still, poised on the brink of heaven.

She trembled and tried to pull him toward her. "Yes."

He eased in a fraction, but no more. "I think you're aching for me."

"Yes." Her grip tightened.

"Ask me for it."

Her breath caught. "Please."

"Beg me."

"Please."

He shoved deep and she cried out, convulsing around him, arching into her first climax, bathing him with her nectar. He began thrusting, fast and hard, riding the crest of her orgasm as she gasped his name over and over.

She sank back to the mattress, the tremors fading. Panting, she gazed up at him, her eyes wild, her skin damp, her body shaking.

He slowed his movements, but didn't stop. "Again." He threw it out as a challenge, wondering if she'd tell him no.

She sucked in a breath, but she didn't disagree. She wanted adventure, this lover of his. Still locked inside her, he sat back, slipped his hands under her knees, and brought her legs up until her feet rested on his shoulders.

Her eyes widened, and then she smiled and looked him over. She seemed to take it all in—his hat, his heaving chest glistening with sweat, and the place where his cock was buried deep inside her. "Love the view."

His gaze swept downward. "Me, too." As he began a slow, easy rhythm, he was treated to the quiver of her breasts each time he pushed home, and the erotic sight of his cock moving in and out as he created the connection they both craved.

She flattened her palms against the mattress and lifted to meet each stroke. Her breathing quickened. She was getting close. He could see it in her eyes, feel it in the way she shuddered.

Reaching between her thighs, he massaged her pressure point with his thumb. She moaned and contracted around his aching cock. Then her body tightened, lifted and hurled her into another climax that made her yell and tested his control almost beyond endurance.

Yet he controlled himself. Gently lowering her feet,

he eased back down so they were face-to-face, chest to chest. "Wrap your legs around me."

She was still breathing hard, still quaking from aftershocks, but she did as he asked. Then she put her arms around him, too.

He settled in, his hips between her thighs and his cock securely locked in place. He stayed like that, letting her catch her breath, letting him curb his urge to come.

At last her breathing slowed and he didn't feel quite so much like a rocket about to launch. Looking into her eyes, he saw a reflection of his own turbulent thoughts. He had to believe that she wanted what he wanted, a chance to explore what they'd found together. But she seemed afraid to hope.

Maybe, if he loved her well enough, he could change that. He combed her hair back from her face. "I'm takin' off the hat."

"Okay." Her tiny smile said that she understood. Enough was enough. "I'll do it." Reaching up, she lifted it from his head and laid it brim-side up on the bed next to them. "Thank you for indulging me."

"It was my pleasure, ma'am." Leaning down, he feathered a kiss against her lips as he began to move.

Her breath was warm against his mouth. "I don't think so. You haven't come, yet."

He ran his tongue over her lower lip as he accelerated just a little. Damn, but loving her felt good. "I get pleasure when I give it to you."

"Then it's my turn to give you some." She rose to meet his next thrust.

He liked that a whole lot. The climax he'd been holding back shouldered its way forward, demanding to be turned loose. "I was thinkin' we'd give some to each other."

"Maybe." She matched his rhythm. "But this one's for you."

Lifting his head, he gazed into her eyes as he moved faster. "For us."

Moisture gathered in her eyes. "Drake…"

"Shh. It'll be fine, darlin'." He kissed her again, so softly, even though his body strained toward release. "It'll be just fine." Then he watched her eyes as he pushed home again, and again, and again.

At last he saw flames leap in those dark depths and her body began to hum beneath his. "That's it. Let go."

"Oh, Drake. *Drake.*" Closing her eyes, she came apart in his arms. Tears leaked from the corners of her eyes as she came in a rush.

Her contractions rolled over his cock, dragging him closer, and closer… Now. *Now.* With a bellow of surrender, he drove into her one last time and came harder than he ever had in his life. As he held on to her and gasped for breath, he was sure of only one thing.

He'd found what he wanted with Tracy, and he wouldn't give that up without a fight.

Tracy decided to take Drake's advice to heart and live in the present. And the present was darned good as they turned Dottie and Sprinkles loose in the pasture the next morning. A few feet away from the mare and foal, Tracy stood beside Drake, smartphone at the ready, watching to see what mother and son would do.

The foal seemed a little dazed by the grass and the sunlight and stood quietly for a moment looking bewildered. He took a few steps, and when that went well, he walked a little faster. Dottie followed as Sprinkles' fast walk became a trot. Then, as if he'd determined that being outside was fun, he took off running, his little tail held high. His mother chased after him, dodging and weaving whenever Sprinkles abruptly changed direction.

"Oh, my gosh!" Laughing with delight, Tracy turned on the video feature and followed the little guy with her phone. "He's so stinkin' *cute.*"

"When you're right, you're right. Look at him go! He's trying to outrun her, the little squirt." Drake sounded like a proud parent.

Tracy kept filming. "Now I don't know which I love more, the moment Dottie gave birth, or right now, when that baby finally gets out in the world."

"They're both damned special."

"Yep." Tracy lowered the phone when Sprinkles took a break to nurse. "How would you feel about inviting Jerry Rankin over to see them?"

"That's up to you."

"I don't know." She glanced at him and smiled. "Love that hat."

"So you've said."

"I feel as if Jerry should see this. But if I invite him, he might decide to drop by more often, and then…"

"Goodbye, privacy."

"Yes. Maybe I won't invite him yet."

"That's fine, but I should warn you that I made a couple of calls while you were in the shower."

"You did?" She could guess whom he'd called. "And?"

"Regan said he and Lily were fine with inviting Jeannette out here, and Jeannette is checking into flights."

"That's great!" She hoped that sounded sincere. She wanted it to be sincere.

He studied her. "Is it?"

"Of course it is." She almost wished he hadn't bought the hat after all. That thought was unworthy of her, but damn it, Jeannette would love his new look. What woman wouldn't? "You three need to patch things up."

"I agree, but… Listen, Jeannette is a good friend. That's *all*."

"I know! And it's wonderful that she's planning to fly out here." She desperately wanted to change the subject. "Did Regan say when they'd be coming home?"

"Yeah, they decided not to stay longer, after all. Turns out he'd already heard about the mare and foal. And us."

"Oh." Tracy sought out the frolicking colt, hoping the sight would lift her suddenly sagging spirits. It did, at least for a couple of seconds. "From Morgan, I assume."

"Yep."

She glanced back at Drake. "How come you didn't tell me all this sooner? I've been out of the shower for a good thirty minutes."

"You were so excited about lettin' Dottie and Sprinkles out, and I didn't want to spoil that moment with…

whatever's going on. I'm really not sure what *is* going on between you and me, to be honest."

"Was Regan upset about any of it?"

"Didn't seem to be."

"But still, they're coming home instead of staying."

"He said they should do that, anyway. The Chances are hosting an engagement party for them next week-end, and they decided it wasn't cool to sail in on the eve of the party."

"Oh, right. I forgot about that. Well, then. Regan and Lily will be back in four days. Did…did Jeannette say when she might arrive?" She hated that she'd stumbled with that question.

His calling Jeannette had been her brilliant idea, too. Talk about shooting herself in the foot. He might end up back with Jeannette, but she'd been hoping for several more days alone with him before forcing her-self to give him up.

"She'll have to get a few things under control at the firm, so she estimated the soonest she could be here was day after tomorrow."

Tracy's time with Drake was shrinking by the sec-ond. "What sort of firm? I don't think anyone ever told me what she does."

"She's a lawyer. A very good one, in fact."

Of course she was a crackerjack lawyer, damn it. No doubt she was stunningly beautiful, too, and Tracy was officially jealous as hell. Pulling herself up short, she vowed to stop letting negative thoughts get the bet-ter of her.

Jeannette might well be perfect for Drake. She could

help him with any legal issues when he set up his equine rescue in Virginia. She'd also have valuable contacts with wealthy people who might contribute money to the cause.

She dredged up her best smile for Drake. "I look forward to meeting her."

"I want you to. Then you can see for yourself that we're just friends. What happened between us shouldn't have. I hope that we can—" The rumble of a powerful pickup cut into the quiet of the summer morning. Drake glanced toward the front gate. "Looks like somebody's payin' us a visit."

Tracy turned as a cherry-red dually truck drove into the yard. And the morning had started out with such promise before it took a nosedive. She didn't feel even slightly ready to face the man who drove that truck. She sighed.

"I take it you know who it is?"

"Unfortunately, I do. I suppose after telling Morgan and Gabe about us last night, I should have expected this."

"Who is it?"

"Jack Chance."

15

DRAKE STRAIGHTENED HIS SHOULDERS. "I've heard plenty about the guy. It's about time I met him." He was glad Tracy had talked him into the hat. As they walked toward the big red truck, he pulled the brim a little lower over his eyes. He was willing to bet that Jack Chance wore a black hat.

Had he had someone to take that wager, he would have won it. Jack climbed down from the cab wearing a hat that looked remarkably like Drake's. So Jack had good taste.

Instead of coming toward them, Jack rounded the front bumper and opened the passenger door. Drake had never been so glad to see anyone as he was to see Josie getting out of the passenger side. Then again, he hadn't followed the program. He'd slept with Tracy. Josie might not be on his team anymore.

As Josie and Jack walked toward them, Drake couldn't help thinking of the gunfight at the OK Corral. Josie and Jack weren't smiling—never a good sign.

Then Drake remembered how Tracy had handled the encounter with Morgan and Gabe. He would behave like the Southern gentleman he'd been trained to be, with a slight Western twist now that he had a hat.

He smiled and held out his hand to Jack as if he'd known him for years. "I'm real glad you two came by. We just let Dottie and her foal out in the pasture. You might want to take a look. He's cute as the dickens."

Jack shook his hand without missing a beat. His grip was strong but not a bone-crusher. "We'd be happy to. Nothing like a newborn colt to make a person smile." But Jack was not smiling.

Josie was, though. "I can hardly wait to see him." She wore a brown Stetson and her blond hair was gathered into a single braid as it had been when Drake had talked with her.

He couldn't believe that had been a mere two days ago. It felt as if months had passed since then.

"That's one of the reasons we're here," Josie said. "Let's go see the little guy."

Drake took note that it was only *one of the reasons*. He exchanged a quick glance with Tracy before they all walked back up to the pasture. She shrugged.

"The place is coming along." Jack looked around as he and Josie walked a little ahead of Drake and Tracy.

"I didn't see it before the transformation," Drake said, "but Regan told me about the work everyone did to make it a viable operation."

"Regan and Lily get most of the credit," Josie said. "They worked so hard, and I'm glad they took this trip.

They both deserve a break from the routine. I'm glad you were available to house-sit for them, Tracy."

"Me, too, although they may not thank me for taking in a pregnant mare."

Jack cleared his throat. "That's one of the things I want to talk to you about."

"That I overstepped my authority? I know that I—"

"She had no choice." Drake spoke without hesitation. "She was faced with an animal in dire straits. She did the right thing."

Jack glanced at him, and for the first time he *almost* smiled. "Easy, Brewster. I wasn't criticizing her decision. I absolutely agree it was the right one. If there's any blame, it belongs to Jerry Rankin. I'm trying to decide whether he deserves the job I've given him. He put Tracy in a helluva position. Nice hat, by the way. Looks new."

"Thanks. It is." And that, Drake thought, was why Jack Chance was the reigning prince around here. He projected authority with his big red truck and his take-charge attitude, but then, just when you were ready to hate the guy for throwing his weight around, he disarmed you with an obviously sincere compliment about your new hat.

Josie had mentioned that she thought Drake and Jack would get along. Drake wasn't sure about that, but it would be interesting to find out. Much depended on Jack's other reasons for driving over to Peaceful Kingdom. At least Drake had put him on notice that nobody was going to chastise Tracy while he was around.

"Jerry's a poor old guy who ended up in a bad situation," Tracy said. "Do you know he can't read?"

"I found that out." Jack paused as they reached the pasture fence. Then he leaned on it and gazed at Dottie chasing after Sprinkles. "Now that's a real good-looking horse. If her foals typically looked like that one, I can see why Jerry made some money."

Tracy joined him at the fence. "But if his wife was his business manager, after she died he couldn't handle things the way he used to. I think she helped him disguise his illiteracy so he could keep his job and sell Appaloosas on the side."

Drake admired the way she stuck up for Jerry. Her compassion was another thing he loved about her. The list kept growing.

Jack nodded. "Yeah, I think that's true. I'm just not sure he's the right fit for the Last Chance. I'll keep him on for a while, but he's a little overwhelmed by the size and scope of the place. However…" He turned and leaned his back against the fence and propped one booted foot on the bottom rail as he surveyed Peaceful Kingdom.

Tracy smiled. "Nice try, but you're talking to the wrong person. Regan and Lily have to make that decision."

"She's right, Jack," Josie said. "Don't go trying to strike a deal with Tracy. Honestly. You would have made a great politician."

Jack didn't disagree. "Hey, she's met the guy. She could be his character reference."

Drake couldn't help laughing at that. "Wouldn't you

be the logical character reference? She saw Jerry for about twenty minutes, tops. He's workin' at your ranch. You know him better than she does."

"Yes, but if I talk him up, Regan and Lily will figure out I'm trying to unload him, which I am. Whereas Tracy has nothing to gain or lose if she talks him up. She'll have a much better chance of convincing them to take on Jerry than I will. They'll suspect me of ulterior motives."

Josie shook her head. "Which you have coming out your ears. So, are we done with this topic?"

"That depends." Jack glanced at Tracy. "Will you please put in a good word for old Jerry with Regan and Lily?"

She grinned at him. "Yes, Jack, I will. I really think he'd make a great employee here."

"Thank you. So do I. And that frees us up to discuss a more sensitive topic." He looked straight at Drake.

Drake tensed.

Tracy had obviously seen Jack's look, because she pushed away from the fence and faced him, her jaw tight. "Jack, you know I think a lot of you, but if you're going to say anything negative about Drake, then, with all due respect, I'll have to ask you to get back in your truck and drive away."

Drake was touched by her loyalty, but he couldn't ask her to fight his battles. He stepped forward. "I appreciate that more than I can say, but if Jack wants to have it out with me, we should. Maybe it'll clear the air. I'm sick of having the most prominent family in Shoshone treat me like a leper."

"A leper?" Jack looked wounded. "I hardly think that's fair, Brewster. We've been polite. From a distance."

"Which is exactly how they used to treat lepers, Chance!"

"Oh, for God's sake." Josie blew out a breath. "Drake, we came over this morning to invite you to Regan and Lily's engagement party next weekend."

Drake was stunned into silence.

"I was working up to that," Jack grumbled. "Then everybody jumped on me."

Drake still couldn't get his head around it. "You're inviting me to a party…at the Last Chance Ranch?"

"Yes." Josie's tone was friendly but efficient. "It starts at one, and we'll be serving an outdoor barbecue. You can bring a gift if you'd like, but it's certainly not—"

"You bet I'll bring a gift! Regan's my best friend!" Belatedly he realized he wasn't exactly displaying his Southern gentleman's manners. "I appreciate the invitation. Thank you."

"It required a big family meeting," Jack said.

"Jack." Josie gave him a look of warning.

"Well, it did."

"We don't need to discuss it, though."

"Oh, please do." Drake was fascinated. "I've never been the subject of a big family meetin' before. I want to hear about it."

Jack seemed all too willing to share. "See, Morgan was on the phone with everybody last night, carrying on about the incident at the hamburger joint. So my mom,

Sarah Chance Beckett to you, called a family meeting early this morning because she said we couldn't keep this up. Regan's been saying you're an okay guy, and now Tracy seems to think so, too, so we voted, and…" He shrugged. "Looks like you're in. Congratulations."

"I'll be damned." He glanced over at Tracy. "Will you be my date for this shindig?"

To his surprise, she hesitated. "I'd be glad to, but don't forget that Jeannette will probably still be here then. You might rather take her, instead."

"If it comes to that, I'll take both of you."

Tracy's cheeks turned pink. "No, that's okay. I can get there on my own."

He realized that suggesting all three of them go together might not have been his brightest idea.

Then Jack spoke up again. "Who's Jeannette?" He looked from Drake to Tracy. "The name sounds familiar, but I can't place her."

Josie cleared her throat nervously. "Are we talking about Regan's Jeannette? Wait, I don't mean that like it sounded. She's not *Regan's* Jeannette anymore, obviously. But is she the woman I'm thinking of? Because if she is, then—"

"Yes, it's that Jeannette, and I invited her to come here for a visit," Drake said. "I cleared it with Regan and Lily, first, of course."

Jack stared at him in obvious disbelief. "Brewster, I was just thinking that maybe I might like you, and now I discover to my great disappointment that you have shit for brains. Are you telling me that you have invited Regan's ex-fiancée to Jackson Hole?"

"It was my idea," Tracy said. "Well, not the inviting part, but having Drake call her was my idea. They've been buddies since they were kids, and now they're not friends anymore. That's a shame."

"Of course they're not friends!" Jack scowled at Drake. "You slept with her! You can't be friends with someone you…" He shot a glance in Josie's direction. "Well, yes, you can, but not in this case. This is a particularly screwed-up case. You really invited her here? Really?"

"Yes, I did."

"Can you uninvite her?"

"No, I can't. She's probably already booked a flight. She should be here in a couple of days."

Jack groaned. "We're just now getting used to *you*, and you bring the other half of the triangle into town?" His scowl deepened. "Hold it. Scratch that. You can't have two halves of a triangle. It would be the other third of the triangle, but who the hell gives a damn about geometry at a time like this? Brewster, you suck."

"He does *not*." Tracy got right in Jack's face. "I started all of this by saying he should get in touch with her, but if he thinks it's an even better idea to bring her out here so that she can clear the air with Regan, and Regan and Lily agree to it, then it's a done deal. You don't have to meet Jeannette, so it's none. Of. Your. Business." She held his gaze with defiance radiating from every part of her trembling body.

Jack blinked. "Oh." He adjusted the angle of his hat so it sat back a little more on his head. "You have a point." He looked over at Drake. "Sorry, Brewster.

Sometimes I forget I'm not the king. Fortunately I have people more than willing to remind me of that."

Drake was blown away, both by Tracy's fierce defense of him and Jack's instant capitulation. "Apology accepted."

Jack held out his hand and Drake shook it. Then Jack glanced at Josie. "Think we should mosey on home, now?"

She rolled her eyes. "Not yet, Your Majesty. Drake needs to know whether Jeannette is welcome at the party. I'd be happy to have her. I'll bet Regan will want her there. But if you're going to treat her like a leper, too, then—"

"Oh, God. Here we go with the leper thing again." Jack sighed and faced Drake again. "Please bring whoever you want to the party, Brewster." He looked to Josie for approval. "Is that okay?"

She smiled. "That's fine. Let's go home."

"Yeah, let's do. I'm exhausted."

Josie came over and hugged Tracy. Then she sent a cautious smile Drake's way. "See you two later."

Jack gave Drake one last glance. "I really do like the hat. It suits you." Then he slung an arm around Josie's waist and they headed back to the big red truck.

Once they were out of hearing range, Drake turned to Tracy and cupped her face in both hands. "I don't know what to say. You were incredible. It's not even your fight, but you stood up for me." His gaze searched hers and found what he was looking for. She loved him. He knew it more surely than he knew his own name. "Tracy, I'm in love with you, and I think you're in—"

"Drake, you can't trust what you're feeling now."

"The hell I can't. I've never met a woman I've wanted this much, and not just sexually, although that part is beyond amazing. That's rare, by the way. Take my word for it because I'm the one who's supposed to be the experienced person in this group."

"Okay, I believe you, but—"

He tightened his grip and poured out his heart. "I want *you,* Tracy. All of you—your compassion, your loyalty, your crazy fantasies, your great laugh, your quirky sense of humor, which is so much like mine it's scary. But mostly I want that certain something we share, as if we've known each other forever, as if we *will* know each other forever. I want to be with you, Tracy. Whatever it takes, I want to be with you."

"Oh, Drake…" Her eyes grew moist. "I wish it could be that simple."

"It is simple. We'll make it that way. We'll—damn, there's my phone." And it was Jeannette's ring. Terrible timing. He decided to let it go to voice mail.

But Tracy gently took his hands from her face and stepped away from him. "Take the call. It might be Jeannette."

"I don't care. I'll get it later."

"Take the call."

The moment was spoiled, anyway, so he reached for the phone in his pocket. It had stopped ringing, but then his text message signal chimed. He opened the message. When he lifted his head, Tracy was watching him, a question in her eyes.

He knew the news would mean their time alone was

pretty much over. "Jeannette finished work ahead of schedule and she's flying in tonight. Come with me to the airport. I want her to meet you. I want her to meet the woman I—"

"No, Drake." She shook her head. "For one thing, I have to work tonight. For another, you two need time alone."

"We can talk on the way back from the airport. I'll come by Spirits and Spurs."

"Please don't." Panic gripped her. She didn't want to face what could end up being the love of Drake's life while she was in a public situation where she couldn't escape. "She'll be tired, and I'll be busy. It wouldn't be a good beginning for either of us."

"I guess not."

"Just take her back to your cabin. I'll meet her…later. Now let's go round up the horses and put them back in the barn before Sprinkles wears Dottie to a frazzle."

He agreed, and while they did, he found himself regretting that he'd invited Jeannette to Jackson Hole. Maybe it would end up okay, but he had a bad feeling that her visit threatened to ruin everything.

16

TRACY THOUGHT SHE'D prepared herself to get through this night. She'd worked especially hard at Spirits and Spurs and had even stayed later than she needed to while she polished every item behind the bar until the area gleamed. She would hear from Drake the next day, and that was fine.

He and Jeannette had plenty to talk about. They'd stay up late, so he wouldn't come back to Peaceful Kingdom in the middle of the night. But just in case, she left the front door unlocked because she'd never given him a key.

She was almost sure he wouldn't come over, though. He and Jeannette would both be tired from the emotional stress of seeing each other and working through their issues. She couldn't really believe he would just leave Jeannette and come back here.

Logically, he'd offer her his bed in the cabin, and… he'd take the sofa. Tracy did her best to picture Drake on that sofa, but the image of them sharing a bed wouldn't go away, no matter how she tried to banish it.

Drake had claimed to love her, although she was afraid to believe it. But if *he* believed it, then he wouldn't share a bed with Jeannette, not even just to sleep. Or would he? Tracy thought of how long Drake and Jeannette had been friends. If you knew someone that well, would you even think twice about sleeping in the same bed? Maybe not. And it would be *fine*.

No, it wouldn't, damn it. She didn't want any other woman waking up beside Drake, whether they'd had sex or not. She slept in Regan and Lily's king-size bed that night, unwilling to stay in the room that contained so many hot memories of Drake.

Or rather, she *didn't* sleep. All she could do was lie there and stare into the darkness, torturing herself as she wondered what was happening in Drake's cabin. She'd never spent such a miserable night in her life.

Finally, when it was barely light out, she crawled out of bed, dressed in old jeans and a T-shirt, and staggered into the kitchen to make coffee. She might as well jack herself up with caffeine, because today didn't promise to be any better, stress-wise, and coffee would have to substitute for sleep.

As the coffee brewed, she paced the kitchen in her bare feet and reminded herself that no one was to blame for her misery except her. She'd taken in the pregnant mare against orders. She'd elected to call Drake, and then she'd invited him to stay.

Oh, but it got worse. She'd initiated the sex. If she hadn't gone to the barn that night, he wouldn't have made the first move. Not with all the guilt he'd carried about Regan and Jeannette.

Tension would have remained high, but they wouldn't have spent all that lovely time in bed together. She wouldn't have taken him hat shopping. She wouldn't have fallen in love with him. She didn't regret any of it, but man, payback was a bitch.

She was pouring her first cup of coffee when the front door opened. Her stomach pitched. If he'd brought Jeannette over here without warning her, without giving her a chance to shower and fix her hair and put on makeup, she'd *kill* him.

Heart pounding, she finger combed her unbound hair and tugged down the hem of her T-shirt, but she was positive that she looked like hell. Couldn't be helped.

He walked into the kitchen looking at least as ragged as she felt, although he had one thing going for him. He'd worn his hat. But he was in desperate need of a shave, and his Western shirt—the same one he'd left in—was badly wrinkled. He regarded her through bloodshot eyes, and his voice was hoarse, as if he'd used it a lot in the past few hours. "I love you."

She felt as if a gigantic vacuum had sucked the air out of the room. "Drake, you may think—"

"I don't *think,* Tracy. I *know.* Just like I know you love me, but I don't want to stand here and argue about it. Put somethin' on your feet. We're taking a ride."

She struggled to breathe. "Who's we? Is Jeannette with you?"

"No. She's asleep in the cabin."

Okay. That helped. She took a shaky breath.

"We stayed up most of the night talkin'—about us, about Regan, but mostly about you." He sounded tired. "I was pretty damned sure how I felt, but after all those hours of goin' over it with Jeannette, every doubt is gone. Go get your shoes. Or your boots. Whatever."

"Where are we going?"

"I'll tell you on the way."

"There's coffee if you want some." She gestured to the pot.

"That'll be nice to have, at that. I'll fix us a thermos."

"I'll be right back." She hurried into the bedroom and put on some sneakers. Her boots had a strong association for him, and she didn't want to cloud the issue of whether he was in love with her by causing him to think about sex.

When she returned to the kitchen, he picked up the thermos. "Let's go. We need to be back in time to feed the critters."

She nodded. Whatever he was up to, he seemed to have taken all the factors into consideration. He helped her into his dusty black SUV, but that was the only time he tried to touch her. He behaved like a man on a mission, a man who wouldn't allow himself to be distracted until he'd achieved his goal.

This was a side of Drake she'd never seen before. He'd always seemed so laid-back with his Southern accent and his tendency to joke about nearly everything. That Drake wasn't driving the SUV and pushing the speed limit. Fortunately nobody else was on the road at this hour.

To her surprise, he seemed to be going toward the

Last Chance. But that would also take them past the cabin where Jeannette lay sleeping. "You're not taking me to see Jeannette, are you? Because I'd rather not go over there looking like I'd been pulled backward through a knothole, and I'm sure she wouldn't appreciate seeing me before she has a chance to—"

"I'm takin' you to a place Josie mentioned to me a while ago. After you and I came to an impasse yesterday, I called her and got directions. I wasn't sure whether I'd need them or not, but it seemed like a good plan to have in my hip pocket."

"Are we going to that flat rock, the one that's supposed to be sacred to the Shoshone tribe?"

"That's it. Have you been there?"

"No. It's on Chance land, so I'd have to ask first, and I just never... To tell you the truth, I would have felt funny telling them I wanted to go stand on their rock to clear my mind."

"You have my permission to feel as funny as you want, because that's exactly what we're gonna do. I'm runnin' out of ways to convince you that what we have is the real deal, so we'll give this a shot."

"You're, um, driving kind of fast."

"I want to get there before the sun comes up."

"Okay." She settled back in her seat and decided not to talk to him for the rest of the trip. If he insisted on barreling down the highway, she didn't want to interfere with his concentration. "I'll watch for cops."

"Thanks." He floored it, and they came to the Last Chance turnoff in no time at all.

The road was unpaved and known for being an axle-breaker, so he slowed down. Drake swore each time the SUV bottomed out. "Jack needs to maintain his damned road."

"He leaves it this way on purpose."

"You're kiddin' me."

"No. It's how his father chose to discourage trespassers. Other family members take a different view, and they've argued about it for years. It's still like this, so I guess Jack's winning."

"Bully for him." Drake hit another pothole and cussed again. "Wouldn't hurt to have a few lights out here, either."

Tracy smiled. Drake was used to the manicured pastures and well-maintained roads of Virginia farms. He was wearing an awesome Western hat and he had fully subscribed to the cowboy code of honor, but at heart he was a Southern gentleman. She cherished that about him. It was part of who he was.

But she wasn't questioning her feelings for him. He thought he could convince her of his sincerity by standing on a piece of granite at sunrise. It was the kind of scenario that would appeal to the soul of a poet. She cherished that about him, too.

They rounded a curve and the ranch buildings came into view. Drake whistled under his breath and slowed down. "Now that's impressive." He brought the SUV to a stop and switched off the headlights.

"Uh-huh." In the predawn light, the immense two-story log house loomed even bigger than in broad daylight. Faint light glowed in a couple of the windows. The occupants might be starting their day.

"I like the way the wings are angled." Drake leaned on the steering wheel and peered at the house. "Like they're welcomin' you to come and sit a spell."

"I think so, too. Jack's grandparents started with just that center section, and then the two wings were added later. My favorite part is the porch that runs the length of the whole thing."

"Mine, too. The rockers remind me of porches in the South."

"People sit on porches out here, too."

"Obviously." Drake's gaze took in the rest of the buildings, which included the original barn, the tractor barn, the bunkhouse and several corrals. "Quite an operation. Probably worth millions."

"It is, but they have no plans to sell, and the overhead has to be huge. Josie says that Jack works hard to make sure the place stays in the black."

"I can believe it." Drake looked at Tracy. "But fascinatin' as all that is, we have a date with the sun." Stepping on the gas, he turned left and followed another dirt road that wound westward through ranch land and brought them closer to the mountains.

He took this road more slowly. "Keep an eye out for the rock."

"I will."

"It'll be on the right. It's supposed to be the size of a parking spot."

"So I've heard. Let's put down the windows now that dust won't come billowing in."

"Sure. Sorry about the wild ride. Just wanted to get here in time." He lowered the front windows and cool morning air wafted in, along with the occasional chirp of a bird.

Tracy drew in a deep breath. The scent of dew-soaked grass and a whiff of evergreens across a meadow calmed her. "Ah. Nice."

"I know you love it here."

"Of course I do. Who wouldn't?" But something in the way he'd said it told her it was more than an idle comment. "To be fair, I haven't been out of the state, so I don't know what other places are like. Oh, I did take one short trip to Idaho with some friends from high school, but that barely counts since it's just across the border."

"If you had to live in just one place, this isn't a bad choice."

"Probably not. Wait, slow down! It's right up ahead! I saw something sparkle in your headlights. Everybody says it sparkles in the light. The quartz in the granite makes it do that."

He slowed the SUV to a crawl. "Okay, I see it. Josie said I could park beside it. The ground's packed down from all the folks who've parked there."

"Can you pull in so your headlights shine on it? I want to see the sparkling effect again. This is cool. Now I wish I hadn't been so shy about asking to come out here."

Drake maneuvered the SUV until the headlights were focused directly on the slab of gray rock with veins of white quartz running through it. "How's that?"

"Perfect. It's as if teenaged girls were out here playing with glitter."

"I'll leave the lights on. We won't be here that long."

"Okay." Tracy reached for her door handle.

"Hang on. I'll come get you. And I'm leavin' this." He took off his hat and laid it on the dash.

She sat patiently and waited for him to come around. He really was cute about that. Even though she was a fully liberated woman, she enjoyed his gestures because he'd never implied that she *couldn't* do those things for herself. He just liked making her feel special.

He thoroughly succeeded at that. As he helped her out of the SUV, she felt like a princess being escorted to the ball. Hand in hand, they walked up to the rock, which jutted out of the earth about two feet.

Tracy surveyed the granite. "So we just climb up on it?"

"Josie said it's supposed to work better if you take off your shoes."

"Then let's do it. It would be silly to come all the way out here and not do it right." She let go of Drake's hand, sat on the rock and pulled off her sneakers. She hadn't bothered with socks.

He followed suit and took off his boots and socks. "I'll go up first." Bracing his palm on the rock, he vaulted up.

"Nice job."

"I was on the gymnastics team in high school."

"There are so many things I don't know about you."

He held out his hand. "But you know the important things."

She thought about that as she placed her hand in his and he pulled her up. He was right. She knew enough to love the man he was and the man he would become.

Once he began devoting his time to equine rescue, he would blossom as his innate kindness was allowed to flourish. She wished that she could read the poems he would write then.

He led her over to the center of the rock. "So, what do you think?"

She paid attention to the feel of the rock under her feet. "It's warmer than I thought it would be." Glancing down, she smiled. "I feel as if I'm standing on the Milky Way."

"And I feel as if…I'm standing…with the woman I'm supposed to be with…forever."

She looked into his eyes and tried to tell herself that he was confused, but he didn't look confused. There was no teasing in those green depths. The self-mockery was gone, too. In its place gleamed the clear certainty of a man who knew what he wanted. And he wanted her.

A burst of energy radiated from the spot where his hand clasped hers. It flowed through her body in a tingling river of sensation. She almost expected to begin sparkling like the rock at her feet.

"I love you." His voice was as steady as his gaze. "No matter what happens between us, no matter whether you choose to be with me or not, that isn't going to change."

Warmth filled her, then, and with that warmth came precious knowledge. He loved her. *He loved her.*

He stared at her, and then he sucked in a breath. "You believe me."

"Yes." She couldn't stop smiling.

"You believe me!" He scooped her up and twirled them around. "Thank God. Oh, thank God." Setting her down again, he held her face with both hands. "Tracy Gibbons, will you marry me?"

"Yes."

"We can live anywhere you want. You love this place, and I want you to be happy, so I—"

"Don't be silly." She wrapped her arms around his waist. "We're moving to Virginia, and we're starting an equine-rescue facility, and I'm going to get my psychology degree, and we are going to have a fabulous life."

"Wow. But I'll give you plenty of time to rethink that when you're not standing on a magic rock."

"It's not the rock. It's you. I told you that you are magic. Drake, I don't care where we live! That wasn't my problem at all! I was just afraid you had deluded yourself that you loved me because I was the person who helped you figure out some things. In psychology they call that transference, and I—"

"Good grief." He smiled and shook his head. "I had no idea that's what you thought. I've heard of transference. I took an introductory psych class as a freshman."

"It's a legitimate concern!"

His gaze warmed. "It is if you love someone so much that you want to keep them from makin' a big mistake, even if you'll suffer the consequences."

She basked in the love glowing in his expression. "That would be me," she said softly, "loving you that much."

"I know." And he kissed her.

It was an easy, gentle kiss, but he packed plenty of love into it. Then he added just enough sizzle to remind her of the heat they shared.

With a soft groan, he lifted his mouth from hers. "I wish we didn't have to leave."

"But we do. The critters."

"One more and we'll go." He started to kiss her again, but then he stopped abruptly. "Oh, Tracy. Open your eyes."

She did and was surprised at how well she could see him. Then she realized why. "The sun's coming up."

"It surely is. Let's watch it."

"Absolutely, after you drove like a maniac to get here in time."

"A maniac? Is that any way to talk to the love of your life?"

"It was kind of exciting. You were being all manly and intense."

"That's better. Manly and intense, huh?"

"Yes, but don't let it go to your head."

"That's exactly where it's going, sweetheart. I may need to buy me a bigger hat."

She was happy to discover that the silly side of him hadn't disappeared. Feeling her world click into place, she nestled against his side as a rim of gold slid over the horizon. "It's a new day."

"It's the best day of my life."

"Mine, too." Then she smiled to herself. *So far.*

Epilogue

JEANNETTE TRENTON PACED the living room of Drake's small cabin, across from the boundary of the Last Chance Ranch. Regan, her ex-fiancé, had wanted to honeymoon at the ranch, but she'd convinced him they should fly to Paris. Instead, they'd had no wedding and no honeymoon because she'd cheated with Regan's best friend. Her parents' nonrefundable deposits on the expensive venue, gourmet food and top-notch entertainment had gone down the drain.

Seven months later her folks were still angry, although they claimed to have gotten past it. Jeannette couldn't tell which they'd hated more, being embarrassed in front of their high-society friends or losing all that money. She'd also shocked them to their toes. Their perfect daughter, who'd never given them a moment's worry, had made a public and very humiliating mistake.

Jeannette regretted causing them pain, which couldn't be helped now. She had offered to pay back the money, but they'd refused to take it, as if they didn't want to give her a chance to redeem herself. Apparently she wouldn't be forgiven for a long, long time.

She had a little more hope that Regan might forgive her, though. Four days ago she'd flown to Jackson Hole at Drake's invitation, and wow, it had felt great to see him and find out they hadn't ruined their friendship, after all. The first hour or so had been pretty damned awkward, but then Drake had cracked a joke and just like that, the tension had evaporated.

In a few minutes she'd face her second big challenge, seeing Regan for the first time since he'd moved out of their condo seven months ago. He and Drake were coming over for what Drake had insisted on calling a reunion. She'd love to believe it could be that, but oh, God, was she a nervous wreck.

It helped that Drake and Regan had each found someone. Drake had moved into Tracy's apartment above Spirits and Spurs, leaving this little cabin available for her. The location was good, if remote and a tiny bit scary. She wasn't used to hearing wolves howl at night or raccoons rattling the garbage cans.

Tracy and Lily weren't coming along for this initial encounter, and Jeannette thought that was just as well. No telling how the meeting would go.

Still, Regan and Drake had patched up their friendship, and she'd almost achieved normalcy with Drake. She had her moments of embarrassment and regret, and she'd bet he did, too, but mostly they'd returned to the easy banter they used to enjoy.

That left Regan, the injured party. Seven months ago he hadn't given her the chance to apologize, or even to talk about what had happened. He'd left Virginia as if his tail had caught fire. She couldn't blame him.

But Drake said Regan was no longer bitter or angry,

and she hoped to hell that was true. She was about to find out. She heard Drake's SUV pulling up, and she took a deep breath.

The sound of their laughter as they joked with each other outside made her smile. She used to love listening to them kid around. She hadn't realized how much she'd missed that until now.

One of them rapped on the door, and she hurried over to open it. For one awful moment, they all stood and stared at each other. Then Regan stepped forward and gathered her into his arms. "It's good to see you." His voice was gruff with emotion as he gave her a tight hug.

"Same here." Relief brought tears to her eyes, but she blinked them away. Crying would make them all uncomfortable. As she and Regan moved apart, she took a quick survey of her ex and smiled. "You look good. Happy."

"I am."

She could see the joy shining in his eyes. "I'm so glad, Regan. So glad for you."

"Yeah, yeah, we're all glad," Drake said. "Life's a bowl of cherries, but let's don't be standin' in the door and lettin' in flies." He shooed them both inside. "We need to pop the top on some beers and get this party *started.*"

She laughed. "I found some Cheetos at the Shoshone General Store." Back in college that had been their favorite snack food.

"Perfect." Regan grinned at her. "Can't beat Cheetos and beer."

And good friends. But she didn't say that. Back in the day, they never would have indulged in sentimentality. She wasn't about to screw up their reunion with embarrassing sappiness. Yet this was her chance to apologize, and she wasn't going to chicken out on that. "Regan, please let me say that I am so—"

"I know you are." His gaze was filled with warmth and understanding. "Me, too. I wasn't the right guy for you."

Her smile trembled. "I don't know if there is one."

"Sure there is. Just keep looking."

"And we'll help scout him out for you." Drake passed around the beer as Jeannette dumped Cheetos into a bowl. "In the meantime, here's to the Awesome Three from U of V."

Bottles clinked and they took hefty swallows of their beer, and then spread out in the tiny living room, like old times. They talked about movies and politics, about what books were worth reading and what TV shows should be canceled for their sheer stupidity.

Jeannette soaked up the atmosphere of good cheer and knew that yes, everything would be okay. Their friendship would survive. As for her love life, she didn't much care about that right now. She had her friends back, and that was more than enough.

* * * * *

Can the Last Chance Ranch work its magic
for Jeannette, too?
Read on for a sneak peek of RIDING HOME,
the next SONS OF CHANCE *book by*
Vicki Lewis Thompson coming August 2014
from Harlequin Blaze!